Cupid's Soldier

The Girl Who Loves Love

by Cayenne A. Rose

RoseDog Books
PITTSBURGH, PENNSYLVANIA 15238

RoseDog Books
585 Alpha Drive
Suite 103
Pittsburgh, PA 15238
Visit our website at www.rosedogbookstore.com

ISBN: 979-8-88925-129-3
eISBN: 979-8-88925-629-8

Cupid's Soldier

THE GIRL WHO LOVES LOVE

Dedication

I never believed this would be possible, that there would be a day when this story I'd written could be published and sold. This book has always held a special place in my heart. It was something I'd written during one of the most challenging times of my life and if it weren't for my family, for Wattpad, and for my best friends, it wouldn't even exist.

My siblings listened to me rant and rave about my favorite books and tried to understand my visions for my own. They helped me feel less alone and they helped me understand my thoughts on how I wanted my characters to be and even inspired a couple of characters inside the book. Then there's my lovely mother, she's done everything to support my writing career. Since I first showed interest in the art form, she's been incredibly supportive and gentle. She was the one who pushed me to send my book to a publisher and I'll always be thankful to her for that.

Then there are my three best friends, who I will always adore, Vince, Sydney, and Andrea. While I was writing this story and its prequel, Vince and Sydney, in particular, stood by me. While my siblings reluctantly gave in because this genre isn't their speed, my friends read it with excitement and tons of feedback. My friend Andrea helped inspire me to get back to doing what I love doing, writing, and she showed me that the books I had written were worthy to be sold. She continuously showed me support and love and I admire her for her strength and kind nature.

Sage, Gin, my cute little brother Mace, Mommy, Vince, Sydney, Andrea, my friends who I haven't spoken to in a while, my therapists, all the people supporting me or who are reading this book, and everyone in Barbados who I love and adore, I'm so grateful for all of you. I don't think I could have gotten to this point without you all in my life. Even the people who have caused me tremendous amounts of heartache, thank you.

Table of Contents

Prologue

Love is the most beautiful thing in the world. There are so many perspectives on the definition of love and so many different kinds of it.

There's Lustful Love: This is when two people are in love with each other's bodies more than each other's personalities. Sex is a vital part of their relationship. But, even though sex is more important to them, they are still respectful of each other's opinions and boundaries. Consent and communication are key in relationships like these.

Family Love: This is a platonic type of love. People in this category trust each other with everything and do anything for each other. They are not attracted to each other and wouldn't date, marry, or have sex with one another. This could be a deep, long-lasting friendship with someone. Keep in mind, being biologically related to someone, doesn't immediately make you a family. A family has to have a certain level of devotion and care.

Religious Love: When a person prays for something or believes in something so much, they defend and honor that religion (or belief) to the grave.

Romantic Love: There is not really a guideline to follow for this one. But this love is when two people or more, whatever you're into, would do anything for each other. They don't want to be separated from each other. They protect each other and care for each other. The people in the relationship are generally attracted to one another, but there are exceptions to this for example; asexual people aren't attracted to anyone, but still, some of them become involved in romantic relationships. You don't need sexual attraction to be in a fulfilling and romantic partnership.

These are just four of the most common types of love. But what they all have in common is that the people in these relationships care, respect, and trust one another. They stick by them, defend them, and wouldn't do anything to jeopardize that relationship, at least not on purpose.

For a long time I've been studying the way that people interact with each other. I've started to pick up on a couple of different things. For example, some orphans believe that they don't have a family. However, that isn't necessarily true at all. You don't have to have a biological family to consider someone your family and love them. Just like you don't have to be religious to have something you believe in and are passionate about.

But, there are a few things that everyone needs to be cautious about. If these people love you, they will not do any of the following: cheat on you, physically abuse you, verbally abuse you, or pressure you to do something against your beliefs and values.

Growing up as a young woman or man is difficult. Nothing in life worth anything is simple. No one is easy to fall in love with and people definitely aren't easy to trust. But what makes life worth living is challenging yourself to fight for the things and people you love.

Every day that I continue helping people with their love lives, I'm a happier person. With love you can't expect anything to be perfect. There will be fights, and there will be times when you feel like giving up. But that's the thing with problems, if most of them can be solved, what's the point in giving up?

Thank you for clicking on my blog! If you have any questions, please don't hesitate to contact me. I'll answer you as quickly as I can.

My name is Seline Winters, and you just clicked on Cupid's Soldier.

Chapter 1

As a girl who's been alone most of my life, I cling to romance novels and movies like they're a buoy in the ocean of life. After years of doing so, I've made my own opinions of how people should be treated in relationships. I study other people's interactions with each other and each person has led me to the same place of confusion: what is love anyway? I've discovered many different types of love, but because I've only ever experienced my mother's... I can't say for certain what it truly feels like or what it truly is. My knowledge about it is superficial and shallow but I still hope to help people with it.

I have strict beliefs about how people should be treated in a relationship, and I stand up for them. Even if that means I'm not exactly the most popular girl in school, I'm determined to fight for what I believe in, no matter what. I'm not as strong as a lot of other people are, but that doesn't mean I can't fight for myself and others. My battles are just... different. It's something I take pride in.

Everybody deserves to be with someone who makes them happy, and I believe that if you don't try and make a difference, nothing will change. Starting the blog for the people at my school was a way I could help people, a way I could change things.

Although, I never thought I'd ever see Austen Hendrikson, asking for my help. He strides over to me and leans over the locker next to mine.

"Sup?"

His dangerous brown eyes twinkle as he watches me place my backpack in my locker. I heard people saying that Austen needed my help to get his sister to date his best friend. I just thought that it was a silly rumor, I didn't think that he was actually going to try and seek my help.

"Getting my books, so that I can go to class. Excuse me." He sucks his teeth and blocks my path, trapping me against the locker. I glare up at him and start to count inside my head. If he doesn't move, I could be late for class.

One.

"Nah, little Sel, I need your help."

Two.

"Yes, but you can't force two humans, with no feelings or even attraction towards each other, together. It just doesn't work. Eventually, the relationship will turn unfaithful and quite impossible to fix. I help people who have feelings for each other, get together. I help people realize that they are in a toxic relationship. I help people who can't decide if their relationship is worth continuing. Not the other way around." I'm actually surprised I didn't get to the end of my countdown before I snapped. Usually, I'm much more level-headed.

Austen scowls at me, his dark brown eyes fixed on mine and his frozen-cold eyes make me shudder. He inches his face close to mine and my breath hitches in the back of my throat. Even with him practically pressed against me, I stand my ground. I refuse to let him intimidate me. Looking at him straight into his chocolate-colored eyes with as much confidence as I could muster, I roll back my shoulders.

"I'm sorry, but I can't help you." I say, and I shove at his hard chest. He raises his hands in the air and backs away from me, and I take that as my key to start walking away from the lockers.

"You don't even know what I want yet, Ms. Perfect. Guess it doesn't matter, though, I'll get what I want." Austen laughs and shoots me a mischievous smile, his dark eyes burning into my soul.

I've never seen eyes so cold and angry in my life. Despite the smile on his face, there's a murkiness clouding his eyes. It's hauntingly beautiful and leaves me curious. A small seed of guilt begins to grow in my stomach. Was I too harsh? Should I have at least heard out his request? The rumors could have been wrong... I shake my head. No. My rules are important, I won't budge on them.

When he walks away from the lockers, I sigh in relief, and continue walking to the first period.

I have my AP English book along with my calculus book. I don't really like calculus, but it isn't all that bad. I don't have to worry about other people's relationships in calculus, at least.

"Okay," Mr. Reynolds said once everyone was seated. "Everyone you all know the drill. No talking. No phones." Mr. Reynolds doesn't let anyone talk in his class during bellringers, a ridiculous ritual that schools have come up with so that teachers have time to finish grading papers.

When I finish the questions, I place my pencil down, and I sigh. I've never really enjoyed being tested, and these bellringers are just tiny tests.

Tap, tap, tap.

I hear someone tapping their pen on the table.

Tap, tap, tap.

The noise is incessant and bothersome. My nostrils are flaring and I'm glaring at my workbook. Every noise in the class, including the annoying tapping is frustrating me. The person is obviously doing this on purpose and I honestly just want some peace and quiet before Calculus. Math makes my head hurt, especially if I do too much of it, so I really don't need the stress. I turn around to look at the culprit and find his eyes sparkling with mischief, a smug grin plastered on his face like a trophy.

"Can you please stop that incessant tapping?" I whisper harshly to Austen. I forgot he was even in this class, he's usually always skipping. Why couldn't he have just skipped today?

"I don't want to." He says with a satisfied smirk. Leaning closer to him, I smile mockingly.

"I don't care what you want to do. You're distracting me from my work."

"Sweetheart, you finished your work a while ago."

"Do you know how to shut up?"

"I know how to shut people up, does that count?"

"I doubt that. By saying you can shut people up, you're implying you're intimidating. When in actuality, you're about as scary as a piece of blank paper." Leaning even closer to him, I smirk. I've never really argued with someone like this before, it feels exciting. He's leaning towards me as well. His perfect lips, pulled into a smirk and his eyes are bright and twinkling. With every word I throw at him, my face inches towards him, and he just mirrors me. "But of course you knew that already, didn't you?" My voice is teasing, but surprisingly not in a mean way. It sounds almost flirty...

"Intimidation isn't the only way I can get people to shut up, Sel."

His face is so close to mine, his minty breath fanning my lips, and my lips part on their own accord. His hands move from the top of his desk to my neck. His fingers traveled lightly up my neck to my face, and then to my bright red cheeks. The rough yet soft pad of thumb brushes over my lips, and I suck in a breath. My eyelids were hooded and I was enthralled by his perfect lips.

"I use seduction too."

He removes his hands from my face, chuckling darkly. How is it that he got me so flustered without even having to do anything? It's weird, even though I'm embarrassed, there's this exhilarating feeling... my heart is beating so hard. Is this what flirting with someone feels like?

Chapter 2

I'VE GOT A NEW MESSAGE FROM SOMEONE ON MY WEBSITE.

> *'My best friend is in love with my sister. He turns into a pile of sap when she's around, and I want my sister to be happy. My sister's had feelings for him before, but now she's somewhat moved on, or at least it seems like she has. What should I do?'*

The question makes me think, it's a hard one. If you know two people like each other and they're being stubborn maybe putting them in situations where they're together more often would help. Also, maybe the sister isn't sure that their sibling would approve, so making sure to be as supportive and accepting of them could help nurture that spark as well. I type out my answer slowly.

> *'If they like each other, like you say that they do, then you need to make it known to both of them that you approve of them. If you want them to be together, make sure that you can give them opportunities for them to have time alone with each other. Don't push them towards each other, though. If you insist, one or both of them could end up resenting each other. Don't worry, if they like each other it will happen.'*

Happy with my response, I click the send button. The poor person must've felt so conflicted. I'm just an outsider looking in and the situation feels a bit confusing. I'm sitting on my bean bag chair, in the corner of my room, with my laptop sitting in my lap, like I do every Tuesday night. Sometimes, it starts to feel repetitive, but I don't know what else to do. I could just let people ask me in person, but I hate doing that and it's mostly because on the internet I know that the person only wants relationship advice and they don't actually want to be my friend. Which is fine, I'm glad to help. But in person, people will act nice and treat me like I'm their friend for a couple of minutes. Only to ask me for relationship advice once those two minutes are up. When people start off like that and then question me for that same advice in person, I end up feeling used...

A sudden song of loneliness swirls around my body and suffocates me. Everyday is always the same, I always end up sitting on this beanbag. I always end up wondering why my life is the way it is. Why do I have to be this way? Why can't he just come back? Why do I have to hide?

I sigh, I'm sick of doing the same thing every day: sitting here on my beanbag, feeling sorry for myself. Standing up, I decide to go out and do something. I slip some shoes on, grab my wallet, and make my way out my bedroom door. The hallway floor creaks underneath my feet, and I wince. It's ten o'clock at night, and I don't want to wake her up. She deserves to have a good sleep.

Tiptoeing down the steps and into the living room is a bit harder than I thought it was going to be: the steps are creaky and the living room floor is really squeaky, but I soldier on through it.

Outside is dark and quiet. The moon is out and the trees are swaying in the breeze. It's so peaceful and quiet. The stars are shining and flickering, and the crickets are singing. I can see the reflection of the moon in our neighbors bird bath and it makes their whole yard look so ethereal.

Walking on the concrete path, I'm heading nowhere in particular. Just like my life. My grades are perfect and my passion for helping people has given me something to do, but I just don't know what college I should go to, or what I would even study in college. I have no idea what I even want to be, and I don't have friends or anybody to help me with my decision. I'm never going to see my dad again, hopefully. Yet, he's one of the only people in the world who's ever understood me properly and he would've been able to help me figure things out.

The street is empty, and for a couple of minutes, I watch the stop light change from green to red to yellow. Sighing, I press the crosswalk button, nothing is going to happen if I just stand here in the cold. Gasping, I realized that I walked all the way to Kroger's. The house needs some food anyway and I don't mind picking some food up from the store, but it's so late, and Kroger's is a pretty far walk from my house.

The red grocery store sign blinks obnoxiously in the night. As I wait. After a while, it starts burning my eyes, and I start to see those annoying little spots you get after looking at the sun for too long.

There are no cars around and the cross walk finally changed to the little picture of the man walking. Slowly, I walk straight into the parking lot. The lot had a couple of cars in it, and there was a guy leaning on the stop sign next to the exit, smoking.

This whole atmosphere is like something out of a horror movie, it's kind of creepy: the dark sky, the empty parking lot, the blinking lights of a convenience store. Regardless, I continue on and make my way to the automatic sliding doors. A gust of cold air hits me as I make my way inside, and I shiver, goosebumps crawling up my arm. I don't understand why stores always think it's okay to blast their air conditioning and make everything so uncomfortable.

The store is quiet, cold, and there aren't a lot of people inside. It's actually kind of nice. Grabbing a cart, I make my way to the frozen food aisle. I open the refrigerators, ignoring the blasts of cold air; and grab a bag of frozen mixed vegetables and put them into the cart.

The cart's squeaking against the floor as I drag it into the canned foods aisle. The aisle was packed with canned everything, but our family never had an appreciation for anything canned besides chicken noodle soup and sardines. So, I grab a couple cans of the soup and a couple cans of sardines, put them in the cart, and head for the checkout aisle.

My footsteps softly tap along the hard floor, the cart squeaking as I push into the checkout. I can't help but feel awkward as the checkout lady openly glares at me while I place things on the conveyor belt. Every time I place something new on the belt, I notice the woman's glare getting harsher. A scowl's plastered on her gorgeous face, and it makes me feel like I've done something wrong. The lady's really pretty, though, even when she's scowling.

She has strawberry red hair and a heart-shaped face, hazel eyes, and she's pretty tall. "Is that all for you today?" She asks politely, even though she's obviously angry.

"Yes, thank you."

"That'll be $15. 63."

I sigh, and take out the fifty from my wallet. Sadly, that was the last of my money, and I'm not getting paid again till Saturday.

Giving the last bit of money I had to her, I shake my head, my brown hair falling in my face. Waiting for her to finish bagging my stuff, I smile politely. She passes me my receipt, along with my change.

Putting the bags into the cart, I head towards the exit. Someone's hand slams hard on my shoulder and I shriek. When I turned around, I was surprised to see that it was just the one and only Austen Hendrikson.

Chapter 3

Hᴇ'ꜱ ᴛᴏᴡᴇʀɪɴɢ ᴏᴠᴇʀ ᴍᴇ, ʟᴏᴏᴋɪɴɢ ᴀᴛ ᴍᴇ ʟɪᴋᴇ I'ᴍ ᴀ ᴄᴏᴍᴘʟᴇᴛᴇ idiot. Which is probably due to the fact that my mouth is gaping open and closing hurriedly like some type of fish. The cart is rolling away, and I hurry to go and catch up to it, leaving him behind. Quickly, I take the cart outside and start taking the bags out of it.

I could've had a heart attack or a panic attack and he's just following behind me and judging me! From behind me, I hear a rumble of laughter escaping from his entrancing lips. I turn around to see him and my breath catches in my throat at the sight of him: His eyes are shut closed, his shoulders are shaking, his hair is falling all over his face. I've never seen him laugh before, but seeing him now, I wish he'd laugh like this more often. He grabs a couple bags from the cart, and he takes a couple from me.

"I'm sorry, I didn't mean to scare you."

Looking up at him, I freeze, his brown eyes look so sincere.

"What do you want, Austen? And what are you doing here at this time of night?"

"I work here and my shift just ended; I saw that you were here and I just wanted to come over here so that I could thank you."

"For what?" I snap, exasperated. Is he just trying to bother me now? Does he like it when I'm annoyed with him?

"For answering my question on your blog. It was very helpful." I gasp, he asked me for help on my blog? Oh, he was probably the one asking for his sister. Thinking back on the question, it didn't sound like he was just trying to force the two together like I originally thought. Maybe I misjudged him… Still though he should've just asked the question on the blog in the first place! Why'd he go out of his way to annoy me at school?!

"Okay, you're welcome," I say calmly. "But honestly, you should've just asked the blog in the first place!" I snap, frustrated. Sighing, I run my fingers through my hair to get it out of my face. "Anyways, I need to start walking back home now. So, bye." I try to snatch back the bags, but he doesn't let me take them. I raise an eyebrow at him expectantly.

Austen looks around the area and back at me, his eyes searching mine.

"I can give you a ride home." He says politely, he looks concerned for me. "It's really dark out and this area has been on the news for a while because of sex trafficking."

I'm really not sure that I want to be in a car alone with him, but I'm too tired to walk, and he seems to have the right intentions. Maybe it's because he's being very kind to me. Maybe it's the soft gleam in his eyes that contrasts with the look he gave me at the lockers. It could be the low timber of his calm voice and how it amplifies the way he's looking at me. Hell, it could just be my own curiosity. Despite my subconscious screaming this is probably a bad idea, I still decided to take his offer.

"Well, I guess you're right. Thank you, I'll take you up on that." I smile up at him and he just smiles back at me, his brown eyes sparkling. As we walk towards his car, I notice that it's a lot chillier than it was earlier. The sky is a bit darker and it seems as if there are more stars in the sky. It's beautiful. Although it's usually always cold outside at this time of night, anytime I can't sleep, I like to just sit outside. Nighttime is always so alluring to me. The dark never scared me, actually, I preferred it. I loved the night so much that, when I was little, I made up this story where the sun and the moon were people. I made it so that the sun was a selfish showoff because it's so adamant about being the brightest. Yet because of that, the sun was always alone. While the moon was kind, and because of that it shared the sky with millions of stars. It's stupid now that I think about it.

I shiver, my jacket isn't really enough to keep me warm right now. When we finally reach his car I squeal, hopping up and down in excitement.

Austen chuckles lightly, and I smile. His laugh, I've noticed, can either be a terrifying rumble of thunder or a beautiful baritone song. I like his laugh.

He unlocks the door and gets in, and I follow suit. He starts the car and looks at me expectantly. He raises his eyebrows expectantly.

"Where do you live?"

"Oh, um, 32 Willowwood Dr."

He looks down at me with a small smile and then he turns his head away from me, focuses on the road, and drives off. The whole car ride is basically just us silently giving each other looks from inside the car. I shuffle in my seat, not knowing what to say to break the awkward silence.

"Why'd you walk all the way from Willowwood to Kroger's? It's a pretty long walk from here."

"I don't know, I just needed to clear my head so I took a walk, and I ended up here. I wasn't really paying attention to where I was going."

Soft chuckles make their way into the car and they seem to speed up my heart with them.

"Sounds like something you'd do, Ms. Perfect."

I'm anything but perfect. There are so many things that I've had to overcome in my life. So many things I've seen that have made life seem cruel and relentless. I'm not perfect. If anything, I'm broken and I'd rather not be accused of being something so completely ridiculous. There's no such thing as a perfect person.

"Please, don't call me that."

A part of my life that I left locked in the depths of my head feels like it's being forced open again by a wire cutter. He's getting under every inch of my skin.

"Why not? You're literally perfect."

I don't answer.

"Okay, look, I'm sorry. I won't call you that again, I promise."

I sigh, but continue ignoring him. We don't speak for the rest of the ride.

"Thank you," I mumble, quietly as his car stops at my house. I grab the bags out of the backseat, and slam his door shut, stomping home. Maybe, just maybe, he's not the only one who's got problems.I definitely do too. I unlock the door and step inside, closing my door slowly and quietly.

He's not the only angry person here. I can be pretty aggressive too. Quietly, I make my way up the stairs, wishing I could just stomp my feet. Anyone can tell that Austen's hurting, that's why he lashes out at people. But he isn't the only one hurting. I open my bedroom door and close my door shut.

He isn't the only one who's lonely. I really shouldn't be judging him so harshly, because I'm so closed off too, but he's so blissfully unaware of other people's problems. He called me 'Ms. Perfect' but there's nothing perfect about me. I'm human after all. My mother barely speaks anymore. My father isn't here, and it just so happens to be all my fault that he's gone.

I throw myself onto my bed and sob into my pillow for the rest of my night. I forget about my homework. I forget about my responsibilities. I just cry myself to sleep, just thinking about how much of a fuck up I am.

When I wake up the next morning, my eyes are bloodshot red. My light pink room feels too bright, and I certainly don't feel like going to school and dealing with Austen or anyone. I don't feel like helping anybody, I'm feeling particularly selfish this morning. But, I have no right, it's my fault that my dad is gone. It's my fault that my mom is miserable. It's because of my own selfishness that my own father is gone. So, instead of moping, I get off my bed and I look at my light pink wall. I wiggle my toes on my soft white carpet, and I make my way to the bathroom to shower. Today, I'm not going to be selfish. Today, I'm going to pretend to be a fierce little cupid, defending love for everyone who needs my help and answering every single question that comes my way. I have to.

Chapter 4

As I walk into the doors of my boring school, something is different, people are looking at me strangely. They're either smiling mockingly, looking at me in pity, or walking away hurriedly. Gosh even the teachers look concerned!

I keep my head held high as I walk down the hallway to my locker, my posture is relaxed and poised. Every single step I make echoes in the considerably quieter hallway, and as I finally make my way to my locker. I gasp. There, on my locker, are four words that make my blood run cold. Anybody who saw these words would just think that it must be a prank or a joke. Anybody who saw them would think that it must've just been some punk kid who did this. Of course, the person who's sending this message probably hired some kid to do it for real but there's no one in this school who cares about me enough to do something like this out of a grudge. I'm just not that important here. What does matter, though, is the color of the words: black and red, the colors of my dad's gang.

"Isn't it ironic, slut?"

Those four words painted in bold red and black, make me shiver in fear. Anyone who's laughing at me right now, doesn't understand the gravity of this situation. This was meant to scare me, and it did. This was meant to send me a message, and it did. My dad is back in town, and he wants me to know. I could be wrong but honestly there's not really anything else it could possibly mean.

Whether he meant my blog or my sudden amazing grades. Everything is definitely ironic. Now as I look at my dad's handiwork, I'm scared for my life. A single tear trails down my cheeks as I stare horrified at my locker. Slowly, I bring my hand up to my lock and shakily twist in my combination, grabbing my books, and slamming the locker door shut. Looking around, I realize a couple of people watching me with sad eyes, including Austen's twin sister, and I run past them as I make my way to class.

We're supposed to write down two things that you like about your partner and two things that you don't, which is pretty easy... if you have someone to work with. Sadly, no one wants to do this with me. I'm just a girl who people would partner with if it benefits them, and I guess right now no one needs or wants my help. It's the start of the semester so teachers try to find fun games to do to ease us into the hard work. This teacher is known for doing a lot of stupid and annoying assignments like this but it's even more frustrating when people avoid you like you're the damn plague.

Austen walks up to the chair next to me and plops his butt on it. He looks me in the eyes, those brown eyes of his are judging me silently. He's searching through my hazel eyes like he's trying to find something, and he won't, not after what happened earlier.

"It seems we're going to be partners."

The way that he's staring at me is scary; it's like he's trying to figure me out. He's looking at me like I'm a puzzle that he's just dying to put back together. But, if I'm a puzzle, I'm one not worth solving so maybe he should quit it.

"It seems so." I say, staring at him suspiciously. He's stepping onto unsafe territory, and he needs to know that. I grab my notebook, flip it open, and start writing.

Positives:
(1) He wants the best for his sister, it's admirable.
(2) He's different from everyone around him, he never conforms to society and he doesn't allow anyone to hurt him.

Negatives:
(1) He refuses to call me by my name.
(2) He hurts people, sometimes people might deserve it but it's not really a good look.

I see Austen writing as well, and it's slightly terrifying. Sure it's for an assignment, in English class, but, I'm also nervous to know what he thinks about me.

He scoots his chair closer to mine, our knees brushing together underneath the desk, but I don't move my legs. Sparks travel up from my legs to my head, and make me feel dizzy. I don't understand why I'm like this. He's barely even touching me, and, yet, it feels so intimate.

He leans a bit too close to me. His lips brushed against my ear, causing shivers to quake down my spine. Every breath he makes feels heavy against me.

"Having trouble coming up with negatives about me?" He whispers against my ear. I take a quick shaky breath and shake my head no. I'm beginning to understand why he's so admired by girls, he's very charming. Just for good sport, I took my pencil out and added an additional negative.

(3) He's way too arrogant.

"Okay, time to share your answers with your partner," Mr. Reynolds chirps. I bite my lip nervously, and turn around to look at Austen. He stares at me strangely, and then closes his eyes.

"Ummm, I guess I'll go first," he says quietly, almost nervously. "I like that you're quiet and smart. I like your hazel eyes, they're gorgeous and..." he coughs. "I don't like that you're determined to hide yourself from everyone, including me. And I don't like that you hate me." He says, a small smile on his face. His smile isn't smug or mean, it's vulnerable. My face warms under his expectant stare, and I smile.

"Well, I like how you're so loyal to your sister, it's admirable, and I like how you are always yourself no matter what society thinks of you." He chuckles and his smile grows.

"Can I ask you something before you talk about what you don't like about me?" He asks, and I simply nod. "I don't mean to be rude; it's not like I'm making fun of it or anything. I think it's adorable. I was just wondering why you're always so formal with me when you talk?"

"I guess it's sort of a way to distance myself from other people. With *you*, though, it's different..." A blush spreads across my cheeks as I look into his deep brown eyes. With everyone else, if I start acting casual around them they'll try to be my friend. Which isn't usually bad, except they usually don't want to stay my friend for long and now with my father around, I don't think it's safe. With Austen, it's different though... If I act casual around him, I have a feeling that I'll get used to having him around. He leans closer to me, his eyes twinkling with something unknown, something that I can't read.

"You can tell me the rest now, if you want," he chuckles, his eyes gazing into mine.

"Ummm, I don't like the fact that you hurt people sometimes. I hate your refusal to call me by my name, and your arrogance can be very unlikable as well."

Austen sighs and leans away from me and he closes his eyes for a second, looking a bit hurt. As he looks into my eyes, I look away first. I didn't want to hurt him, but I didn't think that I could anyway so I just said what I wanted. I have a feeling that if anyone else had said those things Austen wouldn't have cared. If he did care, he would've shouted profanities at them. I wonder what I fall under in this.

"I thought we were making progress, little Sel," he says, bringing his hands to his face.

"I'm sorry, I didn't mean to offend you."

I leave it at that. The point of the assignment was stupid like I thought it would be. Apparently, it was to realize that everyone has negative traits and everyone has positive traits. In the book that we're going to read, Mr. Reynolds said that it focuses on a person's imperfections and how people learn to treat this person with respect, despite them. However, I think he just wanted to use this assignment so he wouldn't have to grade papers on the book we're going to have to read just yet.

The second bell blares and I jump out of my seat, moving into the crowd effortlessly, and disappearing from Austen's line of sight.

Chapter 5

It's Sunday morning, and if my dad were still here, we'd be getting ready for church. My dad was never a big fan of church, but my mom would talk him into going. She had this spunk in her, this fire, and whenever dad was around she just got even more sassy and strong-willed. After he left, though, that fire inside her was doused in freezing water, and that chilling water puddles around her still till this day.

She has trouble going to sleep now, and when she does fall asleep, she's screaming for Dad to come back in her sleep. She never even has the strength to wake up in the morning anymore, not even for church.

Every Sunday morning she'll wake up at around ten-thirty, and she'll start rushing to get ready, but by the time she's done getting dressed, it's always way too late. Our church starts at ten forty-five and it's about a fifteen-minute drive from home.

This morning is going to be very different, though, I'm going to wake her up early enough to get dressed. I know she misses church. She deserves to have some type of happiness again, and hopefully, the church will give it to her. So, I jumped out of bed at nine, determined to make my mother smile for the first time since Dad left. Sometimes, I think that Mom knows why Dad left, which is why I refuse to tell her that he's back. Instead, we need to show him that we're doing just fine without him. We need to be strong. For once, we're going to fight.

Taking steps into the hallway, my bare feet hitting the cold hardwood floor, I sigh. Waking her up is going to be emotionally exhausting, but it'll be worth it.

Soft snores escape from her room, my mothers room used to look so different from the way it does now. It used to be so alive; Dad's stuff used to be thrown around everywhere, but now, the only thing in her room are clothes and jewelry she hasn't wanted to use in years. Now, the room is lonely and sad. Her soft carpet has a grey tint to it and her bright red walls have dimmed in color. Her queen sized bed seems too big for just one person, and I hate how lonely she must feel now that he left.

Every picture of my dad was either turned around so she couldn't see them; or they were removed from the walls. Dad used to remind her of how beautiful she was everyday, and now there aren't even any mirrors in her room.

My mom's black hair is spilled all over her pillows. Her usually tan skin looks pale and sickly. Walking closer to her bed, I feel like crying. Even in her sleep she looks sad, hugging her blanket like she's afraid it'll leave her.

Shaking away those depressing thoughts, I place my hands on her shoulders, and nudge her lightly.

"Mommy, wake up." I say quietly. "It's time for church."

She groans softly and opens her eyes. She looks at me with glassy, heartbreaking blue eyes, and I try not to tear up with her.

"Get ready for church, Mommy." I murmur quietly and gulp. Letting go of her shoulders and walking out of her door.

I walk back into the hallway, and make my way to the bathroom to freshen up, hoping that maybe waking her up wasn't a bad idea.

***

After brushing my teeth and taking a very quick shower, I head to my closet and pick out a really nice dress: a light pink sundress that stops a bit above my knees.

I don't want to be too dressed up, though, so I put on a pair of foldable black flats. I hear my mom's shower running and I decide to go down stairs and wait till she's ready. I walk down the stairs and into our empty living room.

Sliding into the kitchen, I start brewing some coffee. My mom and I have similar tastes in foods and drinks: we both like our coffee black with three sugars.

I sit down at the kitchen table and wait till the coffee's done, hearing my mom's light footsteps heading down the stairs. I smile, maybe we can finally be a normal family. Just the two of us.

The coffee maker beeps, signaling that it's finished, and I go to make my mom and I a cup. When I turn around, my mom's sitting at the table so I pass her a cup.

"Here Mommy, drink up, we have to leave soon."

Taking a sip of my coffee, I let the hot liquid burn down my throat, warming me up and making me feel refreshed and awake.

"Thank you, baby girl, I love you."

Although, I already know she still loves me, she told me in her sleep sometimes, it was so refreshing to hear those three words without her being half asleep. I smile as I stare at her, my eyes filling with unshed tears.

"I love you too." I say as a tear falls from my eye and runs down my cheek, I wipe away the tear. My dad ruined this family and now we're finally getting better. We're finally fixing things.

"Come on, we need to leave if we want to make it for Sunday school, it's 9:30."

So, we head out, and on the ride there we laugh and we smile together. We might be heartbroken, but we're together and that's all that matters.

The pastor preached about compassion and loyalty. He talked about how this generation lacks the compassion we need as a human race. He told us not to let the devil tempt us to be rude and judgmental toward others.

He talked about how a lot of churches and priests have been lacking compassion towards groups of people just because they don't agree with what they believe in and who they're attracted to and how that isn't what God wanted from us.

Mom was crying in the pew, maybe it was because of how much she missed the church, or because of how touched she was by his sermon. We both learned something from the lesson today. I learned that I shouldn't judge Austen so much, it isn't my job and I could be wrong about him, God knows better than I do.

When we got back inside the car, my mom grabbed my hand.

"The pastor was right, I spent all of this time judging your father and wishing that he was the same man that loved me. I spent all of this time hating him. It's time that I get a better job and move on with my life, sweetheart."

I smile, relief hugging me like a warm friend and I throw myself on my mom. We hold each other for a while, crying all the while. Who knows if she'll really do it or not but it's the thought that counts and I'm so glad that she's at least in a better state of mind for the day.

"I love you so much, Mommy!"

"I love you too," she says sniffling. "So much."

A few tears of my own fall and I can't help but hope that nothing will ever ruin this.

Chapter 6

I WASN'T EXPECTING THAT THINGS WOULD CHANGE SO DRASTICALLY, SO soon. I know that she said that she was going to do things differently, but, I guess I didn't think she meant she would start immediately. When I wake up in the morning, mom's awake and cooking breakfast with a smile on her face.

The smell of bacon sizzling on the stove makes my mouth water, and I find myself smiling harder than I have in a long time.

"Good morning, Seline." She chirps with a bright smile on her face. I beam back at her, happy because today she doesn't look dead inside. Today my mother has a smile on her face, and she seems to have gotten a lot of sleep: there aren't any bags under her eyes; her hair is made up, and she looks dressed and ready to go out somewhere. Today, she looks like my mom again.

"Morning Mommy."

I sit at the kitchen table and watch her cook the bacon and the scrambled eggs.

"You look nice today. Are you going out somewhere?" I ask her, watching as she grabs a plate for all of the scrambled eggs, bacon, and grabs another plate for herself.

"I'm just going job hunting; I don't like that I've put so much pressure on you to grow up, I'm really sorry." She sighs, and I move to get my own plate. As I get a fork to get some bacon and eggs, I turn to look at her.

"It's not your fault, you need professional help and I'm just a kid. I know that you aren't completely over what happened with Dad, and I think you need therapy. It's not like you left me with nothing, I paid the bills with the money in my savings account and I get a little bit of money from my blog, though, it's not a lot."

We both take a seat at the table now just staring at each other and eating our food. The salty taste of bacon feels like heaven in my mouth.

"That savings account was meant for you, for college. How much money do you have left in it?"

"Not enough to pay for an average tuition at a private college or an average tuition at a public one. But, it's enough for what I need if I get scholarships, and I know that I can do that."

When I'm finished, I take my plate and scrape the crumbs into the garbage can so that the plate isn't hard to wash, and I put the wares in the sink. Kissing my mom's soft cheek, I smile.

I walk out of the kitchen and start my journey to school. Outside it is warm and sunny this morning, there's a slight breeze but it's comfortable. The sky's a pretty orange, pink, and yellow. With every step I take towards school, I look up at the sky and watch how the colors merge and twist.

The school building hallway is loud and crowded. As I walk through it, people begin pushing me around like a cart. Although it's unsettling, I keep seeing my mom's happy face as I walk towards my locker. I keep envisioning her hair up in a bun and the smile on her face as we talked.

When I get to my locker, I frown. The red paint is still there. Slowly, I open my locker and take my things out of it, trying not to look at the bold words. Instead, I continue my stride to class. I guess I should've known the janitor wasn't going to clean it up. Maybe I should stay after and clean it up myself.

Forcing a smile back on my face, I think of my mom again. Nothing is going to ruin my good mood, not even the man who abandoned us. So I skip to English class with a huge smile on my face. People who pass me look at me like I'm insane, but I could care less. I'm happy, and I'm not afraid to show it.

When I walk into my class, kids are already in their seats — including Austen.

He looks really nice today: his black hair is styled in a quiff, like always, but something is different. The stubble dotting along his chin sculpts his face and makes him look dangerously seductive, that's what's new, the stubble. His brown eyes meet mine, and I shiver as I walk over to the seat in front of him.

We gaze at each other, the intensity of his stare is driving me insane but I don't want him to stop looking at me. Yet, I'm the first to break eye contact when I take my seat. I can feel his stare on my back, and I squirm in my seat. No one's ever paid this much attention to me, I've never been worth it. I don't know how to react to it.

"Okay class, go visit your partner from Friday. We're going to do another little project."

I roll my eyes at Mr. Reynold's very obvious attempt at procrastination. The chair behind me screeches as Austen drags it towards the front of my desk, and I cringe at the sharp sound. His gorgeous brown eyes lock with mine, for the second time today, and I stiffen.

"Guess we're stuck together again." He says, shrugging his shoulders. A twinge of guilt pierces through me as I remember what I told him Friday. I know that he isn't perfect or anything, but I don't know whether or not he's actually ever hurt anyone. I've heard him have serious arguments with some guys, but I've never seen him fight anyone.

"I'm sorry, Austen. You treated me kindly the other day and I was very impolite. I apologize."

Austen smirks, his eyes gleaming dangerously.

"It's okay, Ms. Perfect."

I scowl, and he leans in closer to me. So close that our noses are almost touching and our arms are brushing against each other.

"I'm not trying to insult you when I call you that, I promise. I know you're not perfect, I just—"

"Observe your partners, really look at them," the fact that we were already doing that makes me turn beat red. "Do they seem happy to you? If not, what exactly do you think they feel? Write your answers down."

As we stare at each other, I can't help but feel even more connected to him. We're still touching, his presence is intoxicating and it's becoming so hard to just breathe. I scoot away from him, trying to distance myself from the sparks. Since Mr.Reynolds asked us to observe our partners emotions, something changed in the way Austen looked at me. It's like he's finally understood something that he's been confused about for a long time. He's looking at me like I'm something special, something I know I'm not. As I look into his eyes I realize something I've never seen before in him, loneliness. He doesn't talk to anybody at school besides his family: Corbin, his best friend for so long they might as well just be brothers, and Lissa, his twin. His eyes, they might be smug sometimes, but they're also so intensely sad and angry that they're alluring.

Austen turns to write something down, breaking eye contact and allowing me to breathe. I open my notebook and write down my speculations: He's lonely.

"Now pass the paper to your partner."

Passing him my notebook, and our fingers brush as I grab his ripped paper. I shiver as I read it. On the tiny piece of paper, his messy writing says, "She's lonely." I look up at him and notice that we've found something in common: we're both lonely.

For the rest of the class, we both just sat there in silence, staring at one another. The epiphany that even though we're so different, we understand each other's pain. We share something intense and terrifying, it's hard not to get wrapped up in it. It's hard not to stare into his eyes and wonder just how much we have in common. I'm breathless when the second bell rings, confused and dazed. I walk into my Pre-Calculus class, not being able to focus on anything or anyone. Some time must've gone by but I can't find it in me to actually focus.

"Mrs. Hemmings, do you have Seline Winters? She's needed in the front office to go home."

I grab the open Pre-Calculus workbook on my desk and stuff it into my backpack, sling my backpack over my shoulder, and get out of my seat. I walked out of the classroom even more confused than I was when I walked in. My mom definitely wouldn't pick me up from school, she never has unless I called saying I was sick.

Why am I being picked up? Opening the office door, I see someone I never thought I would see again; someone who just proved that my dad is back for me.

"Xavier," I mumble as the man comes even more into my line of sight. His long hair, gone. Instead, he has a buzz cut. He's my father's right hand man in business, and I assume, with everything else.

Xavier works with electronics, so maybe he helps my dad from getting caught. He's my uncle, I guess you could say. He's my father's half-brother and he's one of the scariest men I've ever met in my life. He's got tattoos all over his arms and piercings all over his body. The man is terrifying.

I just stand there staring at the man who let my father abandon us to become a gang leader with fear. My legs are planted, stuck to the ground, but when his cold crystal blue eyes meet mine, I run.

My heart jumps into the back of my throat as I sprint to the exit doors. I run outside and run as fast as I possibly can. At first, I ran near my house, but I stopped. I'm not going to show him where I live.

He follows me while I run past multiple houses. He followed me as I ran into an alleyway. When I finally reach the part of town with shops, I smile. I'm panting and slowing down, I need to hide somewhere.

I look behind me to see how far away from me he is, I can barely see him. I notice a little tattoo shop around the corner, and I run inside it. Xavier knew me, he used to babysit me. So he knows that I have this really irrational fear of needles and blood. He wouldn't think to look in here.

The shop wall is black and the floor is a maroon red, but the room isn't as dark or scary as I thought it would be. There's a lot of people in the shop that I don't recognize, which means no one can tell my dad where I am, I'm finally safe.

Chapter 7

HIDING IN THE TATTOO SHOP UNTIL DARK WAS PROBABLY NOT ONE of my best ideas. Especially since my mom is probably worrying out of her mind, I'm so terrified that I'm shaking, and Austen just came walking in.

I try to hide from him behind a wall of nose rings, trying desperately not to be seen. But, people are getting tattoos straight ahead of me, and they've probably noticed me cowering behind a wall. I'm not exactly being very quiet despite my hand over my mouth either. My teeth are chattering like the temperature in this room is under zero degrees despite the fact that it's actually quite warm here.

I can hear him talking to people, and as long as he's talking to them, I'm safe. He's laughing with them, not the same deep laugh I hear when we talk, it's friendly. I can hear his rough voice describe what tattoo he wants: the word safe in cursive circled by thorns on his chest. It sounds really sexy, but I just don't understand it. The word safe doesn't really conjure up the image of thorns to me. I watch him as he walks to the chair with another man. He rips off his shirt and I gasp quietly.

Tattoos are scattered on his right arm, and his abs are so defined. His pants aren't sagging, but with his shirt off you can still see his sharp v-line. I want to trace my finger over his abs and put my head on his strong chest. I blush, my face turning a deep scarlet color. I can't keep my eyes from looking at his physique for some reason and it makes me want to die of embarrassment.

I look up at his face, realizing that he's seen me openly staring at his body. His lips are pulled into a sexy smirk and the tattoo artist standing next to him is chuckling.

"Are you stalking me, little Sel?" He asks smugly. I open my mouth and try to explain myself, only to close it again, knowing that nothing I say will mean anything.

He smiles smugly at me as the tattoo artist sits him down. He starts getting the needles and everything ready and I grimace. When he starts drawing on his skin, I cringe. God, I hate needles. I hate that I have to stay here in this shop and try to fight the temptation to stare at his body while also fighting the urge to run out of this shop full of needles, blood, and Austen Hendrikson of all people!

Despite the needle stabbing into his skin, he doesn't look like he's in pain at all. Seeing as he has tattoos on his arm, he's either very tolerant to pain or he's just gotten so many tattoos he doesn't feel it anymore. Either way, I don't know where I should be looking and I'm still very uncomfortable.

I sort of want to prove to him that I'm not perfect; I don't know why I care that he thinks I don't have any problems. Maybe, I just want him to treat me like a person he can relate with. After what happened today in class, I know he's not trying to hurt my feelings when he calls me that but it also just makes me think that he's putting me on an unhealthy pedestal.

Walking away from my hiding spot straight towards Austen, I sigh. He already knew where I was, so what's the point in hiding from him any longer? He watches me, as I make my way toward a chair next to him, and he smirks as I watch him and the tattoo artist inking him up.

The tattoo is already starting to look amazing, and it suits him a lot more than I thought it would.

"What will it mean?" I ask curiously. Everything about his tattoos intrigue me. He had to have been so sure of himself to get every single one of them, and I wish I was that self assured.

"Why?" He asks, raising an eyebrow and wincing as the guy finishes the thorns, and starts on the word safe.

"I just don't understand what you mean by it. When I think of safety, I know I don't think of thorns."

"It's symbolic-" He says quietly. "With every promise of safety, there's also a promise of becoming trapped. Eventually, every place you think is safe becomes your own personal cage of thorns. I want it over my heart as a reminder not to let anyone trap me in a cage again."

Everything he says makes perfect sense, it makes me wonder what he's been through to fight through life so angrily. He's got so much anger and so much sadness, and he's so lonely. But it sounds like he's scared to let anyone in. He's just like me and he isn't at the same time. Lately, I've noticed my feelings towards him have changed so drastically. I'm so curious about him and yet so in awe of him, it's scary.

I keep trying to distract myself from him by saying things like; he might be attractive but he's arrogant, rude, and probably already has multiple girls hanging on his arm. But while I look at those brown eyes of his, I feel myself blush. I feel my body heating up as he smirks at me. Just the slightest look at me, and I melt under his stare.

Maybe it's okay to talk to someone about yourself; he seems like he could understand the things I go through. The slightest feelings of something more than friendship are itching at the surface of my heart. Like poison ivy, if I don't scratch it, it won't spread. I know perfectly well nothing good will come out of having feelings for someone, especially now that my dad is back in the picture. But, somehow, just looking at him makes me try to convince myself that there's nothing wrong with having a little crush on him.

Somehow, the tattoo shop wasn't as scary as I thought it would be but it's still out of my comfort zone. As the tattoo artist finishes Austen's piece, I decide that if he takes me home instead I won't have to worry about Xavier finding me.

"Do you think you can give me a ride to my house?" I ask him quietly.

"If you want me to," he says, shrugging his shoulders as the guy finishes.

"You know how to take care of the tats by now." The tattoo artist says, putting gauze on his tattoo and smiling at Austen. Austen's loud and warm laugh stands out over the quiet conversations and weird music, gaining the attention of a couple people, including me.

"You finally gave up trying to tell me how to take care of them, Will?" Austen teases with a smirk on his face. Will laughs obnoxiously and smirks right back at him.

"Nah, but the pretty little lady you got with you doesn't deserve to see you whine like a little bitch."

I blush and nudged Austen lightly.

"Can we go now?"

He turns around to look at me and our eyes meet. He turns around and looks down at me, his eyes searching mine.

"Sure," He says huskily, taking money out of his pocket and giving it to Will. He grabs my hand, making my heart jump into my throat, and walks us out of the tattoo shop.

Chapter 8

'I have a crush on this girl, she's so beautiful. She's kind, intelligent, and sweet. Thing is, I don't really think she likes me much. How do I get her to change her mind about me?'

Ⅰ STARE AT MY LAPTOP SCREEN IN SADNESS AS Ⅰ COME UP WITH A short and simple response that could hopefully help him.

'First, you need to show her more of your good side. By that I don't mean to pretend to be someone else entirely around her. Don't change the way you are to be with her, it never works out. If she does end up liking that false version of you, then you'll have to pretend to be that person during the entire relationship. Just be yourself, show her the best of who you are, and most importantly just talk to her. If she doesn't like you after all of that, it wasn't meant to be.'

I've been trying to distract myself with work ever since I got back home. Austen's been on my mind a lot since the drive home. I've been thinking about his smile, his laugh, his taunts. I can't seem to get him out of my mind. No matter what I do the ghost of his face floats around my brain like a graveyard. Trying to swat the image of his smug expression is becoming more and more impossible. He seems to have bought land in my brain and he refuses to let it go.

I groan, slamming my laptop shut. Realizing that I'm not ever going to sleep since it's already four o'clock in the morning, I decided to just get ready for school. Being early for school isn't such a bad thing. If I take my laptop with me I can get started on answering more questions from my blog.

It takes me another hour to look like a human being and in that hour I think about my obstacles and how I can get over them. Sadly, I came up with nothing. How can you beat someone when you don't know what their plan is or why they're going to do it? All I know is that my dad is back, he called me a slut, and Xavier went to my school and tried to grab me.

Grabbing my backpack, I make my way down the stairs and into the living room. Writing a note on the kitchen table saying that I've left for school early. Hopefully today will be a good day for both of us.

When I get to school, the doors are locked, so I just sit under a tree near the steps, looking up at the sunrise. The orange, red, and pink colors burst out into the sky like a firework. The surreal beauty has me captured, and because I haven't gotten any sleep, makes a few tears fall down my face.

Something touches my shoulder, and I jump.

"Seline, darling, you're a wimp," a boy says, chuckling. When I turn around to look at him, I'm not surprised to find Austen there, though, I am surprised that he seems to actually know my real name. He's always using pet names so I guess I thought he just didn't know my name. He kneels down so he can be level with me and those brown eyes stare into my soul, catching my body on fire.

"Because I notice beautiful things?" I ask in a whisper, he leans in closer to me, our lips almost brushing. "I'm noticing something beautiful right now and you don't see me crying." He whispers back at me with a little smirk on his face.

I glance down at his lips, and bite my own. His lavish lips look soft and inviting, and I watch as they part. I gulp, looking back into his eyes only to find them gazing down at my mouth. My mouth suddenly feels dry, and as I look at him, I lick my lips. He leans in closer to me, brushing our lips together.

"Baby, if you want to kiss me, you should just say so." He whispers huskily, swiftly moving his lips to my ear and biting it.

I almost moan. The red hot feeling of his lips on my ear, burning me alive. His lips linger there for a couple of torturous second, and I forget how to breath. When I pull away, I find my breath again. Looking into his melted chocolate eyes, one more time, before I turn around and gaze at the sunrise again.

"Why are you even here so early? You're never here around this time."

"Oh uh… I got into a fight with my family again… just needed the space after all that yelling."

"Ah…"

I wish I could've said something better. Something to comfort him, maybe? But I just didn't have the words.

"You don't need to worry too much, little Sel. I'll be fine."

He smiles at me, and I find myself melting at the view. I look away for him for a moment and unlike before the silence feels comfortable, relaxing. I didn't know that just being in someone else's presence could be so calming and comfortable. We sit there together in silence, wind hitting our flushed faces, enjoying each other's presence. In that little amount of time, I pretend that it's safe to let someone into my heart. I pretend that I know my dad wouldn't hurt someone who I care about. I pretend that I've forgotten everything that's going on in my life and I let my heart beat race. Indulging myself in Austen's eyes like everything's normal and good.

A couple more students ended up waiting outside the door, until the principal came and unlocked the building. While people walk into the building, we stay there under the tree together. I feel him grab my hand, and I look over at him. He's watching me, his eyes filled with concern and worry.

"Are you okay?" He asks, and instead of answering with words, I squeeze his hand. His rough hand envelopes my own as we look up at the sky. His thumb, caressing the side of my hand, and making me feel like I'm special. As we look into each other's eyes I feel myself wanting to be closer to him, I can't help it at all, I'm drawn to him.

His eyes are so full of expressions and I just want to know what they mean.

"Seline," He says quietly. "Come here."

I scoot closer to him, and he crushes me into his strong chest.

"Can I tell you something?" I nod my head against his chest, looking up at him as he talks. "I've never met anybody like you, ever. You're someone that I really want to be good too. I know that you've probably heard a lot of things about me, and they're probably right. I do lose control of myself, I hurt people. I do. With my family, I'm the same way. I shout at them and I hurt them. I don't want to hurt you. I'm honestly scared of you, little Sel. You do things to me… and I-"

I smile up at him, tears in my eyes, as I see the sincerity in his eyes. I hug him tighter till my face is squished into his chest and I can barely breathe.

"You're not a bad person, Austen," I say to him, shaking my head up at him. "You have trouble controlling your anger, but that doesn't make you a bad person."

He looks down at me in disbelief, and I sigh. It's going to take a long long time to convince him that he's not a bad person, but I'm willing to wait. He's... My friend? And I'm happy to even be near him.

"You're my friend," I say with a nod and a determined look in my eyes. "I wouldn't be friends with anyone that I thought would hurt me. You've been nothing but kind to me: you've taken me home, twice. You've never lost your temper with me either. You worry about me all the time. Plus, you've been nothing but honest with me. Bad people aren't like that." He chuckles, placing his finger under my chin and lifting it a bit so that our eyes meet.

"So I'm your friend now?"

"I thought I made that clear when I declared you my friend about thirty seconds ago."

"I'd love to be your friend Ms. Perfect." He says with a wink, and I punch him in his shoulder, giggling softly. Standing up, I wipe dirt off of my jeans and run into the school building with him chasing after me.

Chapter 9

As I run through the quiet hallway, my footsteps pound loudly against the floor. Austen's loud footsteps and chuckles follow me, and close in on me. I turn and run into a storage closet to get him off my trail. Opening the door quietly, I quickly hide in the dark closet. I hear his feet patter near the closet door and he laughs, loud and husky, the sound melting me like butter.

My knees are shaking against the door. A broom behind me hitting my knees as his booming laughter hypnotizes me. I want to hear that laugh until I can commit it to my memory. Until the rumble of his laugh can be imitated by me perfectly.

"I know you're in the storage closet, little Sel. You chose literally the worst hiding spot ever."

I grumbled to myself and opened the closet door, knowing that he's right. The storage closet is a horribly cliche place to hide, but maybe that's why I hid there; so he could find me.

"Awe, baby girl, don't whine." He hums mockingly at me, taking slow and sturdy steps toward me. His eyes watch me carefully, and the electricity between us has my throat feeling dry like I've somehow been placed in a desert. He takes another generous step towards me, and now, he's close enough for me to feel his minty breath fanning my lips. I gulp, as he cages me in with his body. His arms are beside my head as he leans against me. I look down at the floor, biting my lip softly. His body is too tantalizingly close, yet far enough away that I'm craving it. I can picture it, his body on mine. I can't breathe as a feeling of want, so indescribable and intense, boils inside me like a furnace.

He puts a rough finger on my chin and lifts it up; forcing me to look into his seductive, blazing, brown eyes. He leans his head down towards mine, our lips now brushing our lips together, and all I can feel is soft. It isn't a kiss, there isn't any movement or pressure to it, just a torturous awareness of what we both want. What we both need, each other.

He kisses me lightly, but then pulls away causing me to whimper softly. More, I just want more. I opened my eyes to see him. He's breathing heavily, eyes shut, he looks wild. His adam's apple bobs, and I watch as it moves. Finally, he slams his lips against mine and I kiss him back eagerly. As our lips move against one another, my pulse races for him. He nibbles lightly on my bottom lip and tugs slightly, the action creating goosebumps all over my body.

I moan and wrap my arms around his neck, kissing him deeper. Our tongues find each other, and I begin to feel a pressure in my core. The caress of his tongue, and the warmth of his body, made me feel hot and heavy. I grip onto the hair on his neck and pull lightly. His hands move from the wall, to my neck, down to my sides, and resting on the curve of my back, a fire blazing everywhere he touches. I'm dazed and confused, but I don't want to stop kissing him.

His wandering hands move down my back, down to my butt, and my gasp of surprise only furthers his exploration of my body. One of his hands stays on my butt while he lifts me onto his torso. My legs wrap around him as he kisses me as if his life depends on it. I moan into the kiss as his tongue caresses mine and our body heat merges together. Although I'm loving every second of this, it needs to stop. Everything is moving way too fast. Pulling away from the kiss, I gasp for air. He starts to kiss down my neck, but I push his face away from the crook of my neck and jump off him.

The smirk on his face is almost as seductive as the wicked gleam in his eyes which is almost as teasing as the softness of his lips on mine. His lips are red, and his hair is all disheveled.

"I've been wanting to do that for a while." He says breathlessly, unknowingly teasing me even more. I just want to grab him by his tee shirt and drag him closer to me so I can feel his soft lips against mine again. "I'll talk to you later, little Sel."

I slump against the wall behind me, groaning in frustration as he leaves. Classes are probably about to start any minute now. Teachers and staff members are most likely parading around the school building, getting ready. While I'm just stuck in a storage closet doing nothing in particular, besides daydreaming about the fact that I made out with a guy.

Stepping out of the very annoyingly small storage closet and into the hallway, I can hear the clicking of a woman's high heel shoes. Light conversations can be heard from the opposite end of the hallway, as I walk in the direction of my locker with my head down and silently listening to their conversations.

The paint on my locker gleams deviously; reminding me, once again, that I shouldn't feel the way I do. That I shouldn't kiss Austen again, and bringing him into my life could be a serious mistake. I don't know what my dad could stoop to. I don't even know what he wants from me yet. If my dad knows about Austen, he could use him to get me to do what he wants. Plus… he could hurt him.

There isn't anything that I can do to stop the inevitable turn of events. My father is in a gang, so instead of jumping into Austen's arms, I need to be cautious. Why would he come back after all of this time when he could've just decided to never leave? If he wasn't intending on harming me, why would he get someone to insult me on my locker or chase me during school? Why would he even bother trying to pick me up during school, when, instead, he could just knock on the door and ask if I want to talk to him? I'm going to have to stay away from Austen now more than ever.

I open my locker and take my blue backpack out, closing my locker door shut and heading to my English class. The whole class period, I never say a word to Austen. As class drones on, our legs brush against each other, and I don't move them. I want to relish in the feeling of his touch, just one more time. Even though I want to stay away from him and keep him safe, I want to be close to him. And I think he knows that. Despite the fact that I need to stay away from him, it's getting so hard to. He definitely knows that it's killing me to stay away from him, even though I have to. Every chance he gets, I always succumb to the seduction.

The bell blares loudly, and I bolt out of my seat. As I run away from the classroom, I can hear someone shouting my name, but I ignore him. I open the door to the bathroom and walk in. I walk over to the sink and look at myself in the mirror.

I'm reminded by my eyes that Austen shouldn't meddle with a girl like me. The image of a girl with brown hair and hazel eyes, disturbs me. My own reflection. I have the eyes and hair of my father. While I also possess the body of my mother and the height of my father. I'm a perfect mixture of them both, pure innocence and evil.

I step away from the mirror and start out into the hallway, heading to my second period class with the fakest smile on my face. A newfound determination to not let Austen be put into danger because of my family drama showing clearly on my face.

Chapter 10

I'm outside of mine and Alissa's room, silently watching as the creepy man digs through my dresser. Mommy's in her bedroom, and she doesn't know the man is here. Why is he in my room? Doesn't he need to knock at the door before he comes in? Who is he? What is he looking for?

I cock my head to the side to see my twin sister, Alissa, hiding under the bunk bed. She's crying quietly, staring at the creepy man going through my dresser. Did he make her cry? What did he do to her? No one's allowed to hurt Lissa. The tall man closes my dresser, and starts moving towards our closet.

"Excuse me sir, what are you doing?" I've learned that with adults, if you use your manners, they'll tell you what they're up to. If you're cute, and using your manners, adults will do anything for you.

He looks at me, green eyes hiding inside his hair as he laughs and the man seems almost confused as if I said a funny joke. I puff my chest out and cross my arms, straightening my posture like Mommy taught me. I glare at him, no matter who they are or how old they are, I don't put on my best behavior for stupid, idiots who laugh at me.

He stops laughing, eventually, and moves closer to our closet door, ignoring me. If he's going through my stuff, he's probably a robber; Mommy and Daddy would know how to stop him. I look at Allisa, and put my finger over my lips.

"Don't move." I mouth quietly to her as the man's back is turned. Tip toeing out of the room, I run quietly down the hallway, and into their room.

Mommy's snoring loudly next to Daddy on the big bed, and I run towards them. Raising my little hands towards their body's, I shake them quietly.

"Daddy wake up! There's a creepy man in my room."

Mommy and Daddy aren't listening to me, and I don't want Alissa to be alone with that man. I ran out of their room and back to mine. I see the man grab Lissa and she screams and kicks to get him to let her go. He covers her mouth and she cries under his hand. I rush into the closet and I grab a bat so that I can hurt him! I slam the bat in his legs and he drops Lissa out of his hands.

"MOMMY!" I shout, "DADDY!"

The man stands up from the ground and glares at me. He puts his hands in his ugly black jacket and pulls out a strange looking, black beebee gun.

"HE HAS A GUN MOMMY!"

Loud footsteps bang nearby, my Mommy and Daddy are coming to save me. He fires the gun and I screech, falling onto the ground, scared because the loud noise was really close. When Mommy comes in to pick me up, I feel tired and heavy. My eyelids flutter shut, and I fall asleep.

I WAKE UP STARTLED, GASPING FOR BREATH. I WAS AROUND SIX YEARS old when it happened, and the reoccurring nightmare haunts me, still.

The man's appearance changes all the time during my dream, but the event is always the same. I dream about the same thing because it was the beginning. It was the start of how I became a monster.

I slip out from underneath my bed sheets, and glance at my clock. It's only two thirty; I only had one hour of sleep. Not surprising, I've been diagnosed with insomnia when I was only eight years old. The doctors prescribed me sleeping medication but they take a long time to kick in and I end up falling asleep late anyway. Even when I do fall asleep, my nightmares wake me up a couple of hours later. It's useless to even try taking the pills anymore.

Jumping off my bed, I walk out of my bedroom, and into the hallway. Our house has four bedrooms, there are two rooms downstairs and two rooms upstairs. Lissa and I used to share a room upstairs; Kaden and Kale had the room that I have now; and Angel had the other room, near the living room. Now, I get my own room downstairs; it's close to the kitchen, which I take to my advantage. Kaden and Kale have apartments near their college; I have no idea where they live, I don't pay attention when they talk. Angel has her own room upstairs, next to Mom and Dad's room. Lissa has the other room downstairs.

Slipping into the kitchen, I start brewing up some coffee. As I wait for the coffee to finish, I can't help the scowl that takes shape on my face. It's taking way to long and I want my fucking coffee.

After a painful five minutes without any coffee, it finally beeps. I grab my mug and fill it up with the black coffee. I don't put anything in it, I like my coffee black and strong so it can keep me awake. I sip my coffee and sit myself down. When I sit down at the table, I think about the kiss.

She was just there, her big hazel eyes staring at me. The way that she was looking at me and the way her lips looked, I couldn't help it. I needed to kiss her. I just needed to feel her soft body working with mine. I feel like I rushed her, which I do feel guilty about but I don't regret kissing her. I don't think I ever could, I just wish I had waited till she was more ready. In fact, I want to kiss her again. I want to run my fingers down her back and squeeze her plump little ass. I want to kiss her soft full lips until they're bruised. I want her all to myself. I just want her.

"Austen?" I hear the soft voice of my sister ask behind me. I sigh, I've always had a soft spot for Lissa. Kaden and Kale, my twenty year old brothers, can go screw themselves in their dorm rooms for all I care. Angel is a bitch, and I don't give a shit if that's rude. She's Kaden and Kale's favorite and in their eyes she could do no wrong but she's always annoyed me. She treats Lissa like she's some kind of doll. After Lissa was almost kidnapped, she was very withdrawn and anxious. Angel used to try and take her to big places with lots of people and I was always the one who had to calm Lissa down by the end. I get it, I swear I do. She was young too, but she still acts like that to this day with her. She's just so outgoing and she drags my sister out all over the place until Lissa is exhausted. She's got good intentions, sure, but she's still being a bitch. She's the only one of my older siblings who goes to college near home, but I wish she went to college someplace I wouldn't have to see her fucking face.

"What's wrong?" I ask her softly. She's the only one of us that I can easily be comfortable around. I don't have to try to control my anger around her. Just her presence alone has me calm. I care about her, she's my twin. We stick together through thick and thin.

"I can't sleep, I'm so tired of everyone."

"What happened at school yesterday, Lissa?"

"I like him, Austen. I don't know what to do."

I walk closer to her and place my hands on her shoulders. She better not be talking about that asshole, Jake.

"Jake?" I ask grumpily.

"Jake." She confirms, smiling. "He isn't that bad, Austen, I promise."

I take my hands off her shoulders and ball up my fists in aggravation.

"Then why can't you sleep?" I ask, gritting my teeth and basically growling. He's nothing but an arrogant douchebag, we've fought more times than I can count on my hand, and I've won every time. He's just a punk, he'll talk about someone and act like he's tough but when someone calls him out he gets his ass handed to him.

"I'm not sure if he likes me or not," she mumbles while blushing shyly. Sometimes, it's so obvious that we're twins and then other times, like this one, I wonder how we're even related. She's just so damn sweet and pure, nothing like me.

"Anyone that doesn't like you is ignorant. You're my twin, so you're as gorgeous as me. You're amazing, smart, and if anyone can't see that, drag their ass over to me and they'll learn. Don't let some douche bag make you feel like you're less of an angel than you are."

She smiles up at me, and I frown.

"I mean it Lissa. Promise me that you'll stop letting him make you feel like this." I glare at her, staring into eyes very similar to my own and she sighs softly.

"I promise Austen."

Chapter 11

THE STARTLING SOUND OF TREE BRANCHES SMACKING SELINE'S window woke her up very early Saturday morning. The soft pillow supporting her head comforts her as she wonders about Austen. Her kiss with Austen clouding her mind and leaving her dazed and confused. Seline can't help the new feelings twirling around her mind like miniature tornadoes. With every little thought about him, Seline is consumed with confusing feelings that she's never felt before for anyone. No one's ever made her heart race like he has. No one's ever made her feel so alive.

As Seline snuggles up into her covers, she can't help but wonder what it would be like if she were cuddled up next to Austen. Would being wrapped in his strong arms make her feel safer? Would he comb his fingers through her hair? Would he whisper sweet nothings in her ear to lull her back to sleep? Would Seline finally feel like she isn't alone in the world? For Austen to be safe she knows that can't be with him. She knows that she probably won't ever feel him holding her. It doesn't matter how much she likes him, they just can't be together.

Seline sighs, kicking away her covers; after a while of just lying in her bed, she realizes she isn't going back to sleep. Her small feet carry her into the bathroom, where she cleans herself up. Today, she can already tell, is going to be miserable.

At first, she was just going to sit at home, reply to some comments on Cupid's Soldier, and hang out with her mom; but, now, she decides to go out. She puts on a pair of shoes and grabs her wallet. Her stomach is growling, and she has about three dollars she can spend on breakfast food at Stanley's. It's not an extremely far walk from her house, but she can't say it's close either.

As she walks out the door, she sighs in frustration. The wind blows through Seline's familiar brown locks as a man watches from afar. Sean remembers watching his wife comb through Seline's hair. He hates how horrible his life has turned out. He's now a criminal, in every definition of the word. It's tiring and it grates down on his conscience.

Seline changed so much from when she was little, as well, she used to say that she wanted to be a warrior when she grew up. Her favorite movie was Mulan, and she would giggle every time the little dragon, Mushu, showed up. Whenever Mulan wore a dress, she would scrunch up her nose in disgust. Or when those guys sang about what they wanted in a girl, she would shiver in disgust. It was her least favorite part of the movie. She used to always claim that relationships were gross. Even when she was a bit older, she said that they aren't something you should obsess over. She hated magazines. those stupid relationship magazines. Ha. Now look at her, she's got a blog on the same thing she hated!

If Sean could change the way his life went so that Seline wouldn't have to be involved in his business, he would. He loves his family. But he can't. No one can.

Seline starts walking down the street and Sean follows, trying his best not to be noticed by his daughter. She feels like she's being watched as she walks down the street. Goosebumps rising on her skin at the eerie feeling growing from the pit of her stomach. She starts walking faster down the street, not daring to look back. If someone is trying to follow her, making them think that they can see her isn't really a good idea.

When she finally gets to Stanley's parking lot, she tries to run so that she can reach the door. Someone grabs her, and she tries to scream, but they cover her mouth with a wet cloth. Seline tries to hold her breath as she kicks and punches her attacker, trying so hard to escape before she has to breathe again.

She feels someone press a kiss onto her cheek, and as she breathes in she begins to feel faint. Her knees buckle as she falls to the ground. Her eyelids start to feel heavy and her vision turns black. She knows that this might be the end of her normal life.

She's tied to the passenger seat of a car, when she wakes up, where anybody can see her. Her father's in the driver's seat, like she thought he would be.

This is the first time that she's seen him in years, and she hates that she has to be bound and he has to attack her. His familiar brown hair, firm posture, and bushy eyebrows bring back memories that she wishes would stay buried. She doesn't want to remember his gentle laugh and his great advice.

"Why am I here?" She asks her dad tiredly, too tired to fight the stinging grip of the ropes tied to her armrests.

"You're my daughter, and the gang wants to know that you're not a liability. I didn't want to bring you here, you don't belong in this world. Hell, you'd destroy this world with all of your innocence."

His scoff makes her feel a bit better. At least she wouldn't be there with him too long. But she still can't help but feel sad. Is there something wrong with being a good person? Does Austen think being a bit innocent is off-putting? Ugh, she needs to stop thinking about Austen.

"Why'd you spray paint that shit on my locker?" She accuses angrily, her nose flaring as she glares icily at her father.

"I wouldn't waste my time on something as silly as spray painting your locker, Seline." He honestly found the idea to be very absurd, why would he go gallivanting around a high school to spray paint immature bullshit on his daughters locker?

"You called me a slut!" She spits the words out her mouth like they're rotten. "You know what you did, stop pretending that you're innocent."

He laughs, the evil abomination that created her had the audacity to laugh. If she actually approved of violence, she would definitely punch him.

"Honey, I told someone to let you know that I'm back. You're not a slut and I wouldn't go around calling you one. Sorry to burst your bubble darling, but that wasn't me."

She arches her eyebrow up, confused. Who in the hell was it then? Why did they call her a slut?

"Who was it then, and why would they do that?" She asks suspiciously.

"I'll let you find that out for yourself." His maniacal laugh fills the car as he pulls over into an abandoned alleyway, he grabs a rag and a bottle, dipping the bottle onto the rag. She starts to struggle against the ropes, but the fight is meaningless. The now wet rag is placed over her nose and mouth. She stares into his eyes, glaring, holding her breath. But to no avail, she begins to feel dizzy when she realizes: it's useless to fight against him.

<h1 style="text-align:center">Chapter 12</h1>

I WAKE UP IN A STRANGE DARK ROOM, EVERY BONE IN MY BODY feeling stiff and uncomfortable. I can feel springs poking my stomach, and an itchy blanket covering half my body. I blink a couple times to adjust my eyes to the darkness.

I try to find out where I am so that I can leave, but it's so dark. Stumbling through the darkness of the tunnel I try to find anything that can help until I bump into bars. My blood runs cold. My finger flinches forwards hoping that I'm wrong but when my hand touches the cold metal bars, anger fills my entire being. Did that bastard lock me up!? Am I in a cellar right now!?

My brain races as I realize there's a possibility that I'll never be able to escape this place. I might even die here. What'll happen to my mother? She'll definitely be worried if I don't get home on time. What about Austen…? Will he worry about what happened to me? Will he think I just skipped town without letting him know? Now I know for a fact that we'll never be able to be together and the thought itself has my heart aching in pain. My family has the power to burn his family to the ground. My family has the power to kill him and Lissa with a single touch. There is no escape from my family. I walk around the cell, pressing my palm against the wall, not knowing what else to do. The silence and the chill of the place make me shiver and I find myself sitting down on the cold floor. Why'd he just leave me in here like this? My stomach rumbles and I cross my arms against my chest, terrified and hungry.

Finally someone turns the light on and a feeling of relief washes over me like a wave. I look around only to find that the entire place, outside my cell, is filled with pictures of me from when I was little and my mother and father were together and happy. On the wall above the couch are pictures of my mom and I playing simple games and laughing. I smiled, she looked so young and beautiful in these pictures. Near the closet are pictures of their wedding, their eyes are pinned on each other. My dad is smiling goofily, tears in both of their eyes and I wonder to myself if he ever really loved her. If he did, then why did he leave?

On the wall next to the bathroom are pictures of my dad and I; and on the wall next to the doors are more recent pictures of her, but they don't seem to be taken by either me or my mom. There are pictures of her from when she was younger and in love and pictures of her after he left us.

Was he stalking us or something when he wasn't with us? Why does he have the audacity to have these pictures when he's the one who left us?! He made me think that it was my fault he left so why does he have so many pictures of me too?! Nothing is making any sense anymore.

The basement door opens and the man in question appears. He looks at me with fierce determination, but his stance seems so defeated. Dad's never been one to wear his emotions on his sleeve, but I was a daddy's girl. I knew him better than anyone once upon a time. Or.. at least I thought I did. All he's doing is confusing me, why was I kidnapped like this?

"Dad, what is this?" I ask in a quick breath, trying to gather any little piece of information that I can get.

He doesn't answer right away, but the cold expression remains on his face. Instead of arguing, I walk to the cell bars and I slam my hands against them violently. He has no right to leave me in this cage and then ignore me.

"ANSWER MY FUCKING QUESTION!"

"Manners!" he yells back at me and I pause, paralyzed by sheer fucking rage.

"Don't pretend like you're my father when you have me locked! In! A! FUCKING! CELL!"

"I'm not answering your questions if you can't treat me with due respect. Keep talking like that and you'll stay in there the whole damn night."

I don't say anything in response, deciding instead to quietly glare at him.

"Your mother knows what I am. I wanted to be a photographer growing up, you know. A painter was my second choice, but I grew up in this place. My father wanted me to be the leader here, even though he knew that my brother would be a better choice. He thought that after I got the life that I wanted I would go back into the family business, so he trained me anyway.

"I went to college and made a life for myself. I met your mother in a photography class. She was so beautiful and full of life. She was everything I wanted. I wanted to stay with the both of you, because I do love you both so much, but once my father and my brother died, I had to take over. I had to forget about my life before all of this, and keep my promise. I left you guys a year after my brother died. At first I thought that my half brother could take over, but he wasn't trained properly, and it would've taken years before he was ready enough to take over.

"The reason you're here is because my gang doesn't trust you. When they found out you knew, they wanted you to be here with us so that we could keep an eye on you. That's it. You'll still go to school. You'll be able to go back to your house after school, but we'll pick you up at midnight. Your mother has lost too many people already, I refuse to let her believe she lost you, so we'll take you back home in the morning. For now, just tell her you're at a friend's house or something. This isn't a game, Sel, so if you try to break the terms of our agreement, we'll kill your boyfriend. Understand?"

I nod my head slowly, terrified. What do I even say to that? No? I won't work for you? Then what about Austen? And what about my mom? What would he do to them? My eyes get glassy as I realize, I'll be stuck in this life with him if I don't figure out some way to keep them safe.

"I'm glad we could come to an agreement. I'll get you out of there and take you home. You just gotta' sign this contract first so that I know you won't be able to get out of this." He grabs a pen and some paper and he tells me where to sign. Sadly, I end up signing every dotted line he points to me and then he lets me out of there. I've never been so scared in my damn life.

It's hard to process everything that he's told me, I feel overwhelmed: my head hurts, my throat's dry, and I feel like I need to puke. He leads me up a staircase and into an oddly familiar living room. "Xavier, although I'm not very fond of you calling my daughter a slut, I trust you can take her back home safely. I have work to do, or I would do it myself." I gasp, and look at him. He's the one who spray painted my locker!?

Xavier grabs my hand and drags me out of the living room and the front door, life is just getting more and more difficult. His hand on my wrist hurts as he stomps towards his car. He throws me inside the passenger seat and he stomps over to the drivers. As the drive goes on, all I can do is sit and stare in silence.

Chapter 13

Every day is a back and forth for me: a continuous push and pull of loneliness, guilt, and self-pity. Ever since he kidnapped me, I've been repeating the same routine over and over again. Mom and I both get ready - she's found a new job and I'm so proud of her - I walk to school, feeling like someone's been watching me and avoiding Austen constantly. Afterward, I go home for a couple of hours, either waiting for my mom to come home or for her to fall asleep, and then I leave. I leave inside the car of the man who's been controlling me. I'm nothing more than a puppet anymore.

Every day I feel myself getting weaker and weaker, and it's been going on like this for two months. I'm never allowed to have any time to myself, and even though I still get to post things on my blog, it doesn't feel the same. I'm useless. I'm nothing but average.

Right now, I'm in my English class and I'm trying not to fall asleep. I stayed up all night last night helping my father put away files on his computer, he's given me access to horrible things. The things that he's done, that these files say he's done, prove he isn't the same man I used to call my dad. His excuse for forcing me to become a criminal was that if I'm to be there with him I might as well make myself useful. I've given up on trying to help him realize that what he's doing is wrong. Instead, I'm just gaining their trust. I've been sending files to my computer, and I hope that once I've gained all of their trust I can blackmail them to let me go, to let us go.

If it comes to it, I'll snitch. I don't know, maybe he still loves Mom and I, but love just isn't enough for a situation like this. He's putting me in situations where I can't have a real relationship with my mom. She's finally feeling better and I have to lie to her, it's cruel. He's putting me in a situation where I have to look behind me every three seconds wondering if the people I love will be okay. I wish he would've just stayed away. At least then, he wouldn't have been able to hurt us.

I wonder when all of this will end… I'm starting to think that it might last forever. Will I ever be able to go to college? My life is out of my control now and that's terrifying. Working for a gang doesn't exactly seem like a dream job. If I have to work like this for my father this entire time I feel like I'll lose myself in this depression. The man I call my father has done nothing but hurt my family and I can't do anything but watch it happen. I'm powerless…

He's my downfall and my creator, literally and metaphorically. It's not only sad but it's tiring. Every tick of the clock is a reminder that I have to leave my mother in the night. Every unspoken word as the student's all silently read Pride and Prejudice just reminds me that I can't ever have what they have because of my dad and his business.

I have to be more responsible than every other teenager that I've ever met in my entire life. Guys aren't a priority, they aren't even a fun opportunity. Guys, especially ones that I think I might have a slight crush on, need to stay as far away from me as they can get. And all of this is just more proof that love isn't enough. If you're hurting the people that you love or putting them in danger, staying with them is irresponsible.

Austen might make me happy but my happiness won't last long if he's murdered because of me. He's a normal guy with normal dreams and a normal life, he deserves to be able to live it. He doesn't deserve to be a part of a life like mine.

The bell rings for the second period and I start off into the hallway like a zombie. Every slow lift of my legs takes effort. Every time I blink, it's heavy. No doubt, the dark circles under my eyes are obvious.

"Little Sel!" I hear a strong voice call out to me, and if I wasn't so tired I would've ran to class just to avoid him. I don't bother looking behind me, hoping he'll get the hint as I continue my slow tread to room 1023.

"Wait up, Ms. Perfect! Come on!" Austen runs in front of me, blocking me from moving any further down the hallway. "Where have you been?" He asks curiously and a little angrily, like he already knows the answer. "It's been two months since we've had a real conversation."

"Ignoring you," I say tiredly. "And trying to forget about you." I mumble quietly to myself.

He takes a step closer to me and I take a step back, we continue this little dance until I'm pushed up against a locker. He furrows his eyebrows at me, his body pressing up against me and his buff arms caging me in.

"Why?" He asks huskily, his eyes searching mine carefully. "What did I do wrong?"

Nothing, is what I want to say, but, instead, I just glare at him. This would have been easier if he stopped talking to me and at first it seemed like he was going to, but after the first month, he became persistent.

"You kissed me," I say quietly, hoping that he'll think that I didn't like it or something, hoping that he won't make me explain any further than that. He gets even closer to me, his labored breath on my lips begins to enchant me, and I don't want to move. His lips miss mine by an inch and pass my neck, heading towards my ear. I try not to moan at the feeling. "You wanted me to." He whispers seductively in my ear, kissing my ear hauntingly and I swallow air as an automatic response. Little tingles start to trail up and down my spine as he moves away from me, his lips brushing my cheek.

He smirks at my flushed face, but as he takes time to observe it the cocky glow disappears.

"When was the last time you slept?" He asks me sincerely, his eyes full of concern. Sadly I couldn't even answer that question, I know I didn't sleep last night. Usually, I only get an hour or two of sleep before school. When was the last time I even had proper sleep? I really have no idea. He looks at me pointedly and swoops down to pick me up. I laughed tiredly and placed my head on his shoulder, too tired to object. He kisses my forehead and starts to walk me in the opposite direction of my next class.

My eyes start to shut on their own accord and as my vision starts to blur and get hazy, I can't help but think that I've failed him. Yet, I'm happy he's caring for me regardless.

I hear Austen talking to someone as he moves, he stops suddenly and places on a bed or something soft.

"Go to sleep, little Sel." Austen whispers on my forehead, and I yawn tiredly in response, maybe just maybe he's going to be the person who makes me get through all of this.

Chapter 14

THE MEAN MAN IS IN MY ROOM AGAIN, BUT THIS TIME, I'M ready. Last time, his gun really scared me but now I'll make sure he doesn't hurt Lissa. Mommy wants us to move because the bad man almost took Lissa but I'll keep her safe from now on. The scary man looks different this time but maybe I'm wrong. I can't tell anymore.

"Buttface!" I shout angrily at the man, my lips pulled into a smirk. Mommy said violence is never the answer, but if I don't beat him up, he'll hurt me and Lissa. I pointed the beebee gun at him, the one that I found in Daddy's room. I know that buttface has a real gun, but I don't want to shoot him like he shot me. All that I want to do is hurt him.

Buttface laughs like a villain at me, and he turns to look at me. The room isn't dark but I can't see his face, the mask is covering it. All I can see is his green eyes and his big belly. It kinda looks like the old pictures of Mommy when sissy and I were cooking in her belly. Lissa's hiding in the corner again and I need to distract him so he can't find her again.

"You didn't seem to learn your lesson, kid." The mean man hisses at me, it seems like he didn't learn his lesson either. I glare at him like mommy taught me and scoff like daddy does.

"And I told you that you're not supposed to be in my room. So, you didn't learn either!"

The man laughed at me! He's so rude and mean! So I cock the beebee gun back with one eyebrow raised, a smirk plastered on my face.

The meanie looks at my beebee gun and his face pales. He looks scared, like he might pee his pants any second and I laugh. I make my hand into a fist as I glare at him, getting very angry. Mommy always tries to calm me down when I'm like this but it's very hard. I'm like this a lot now. I'm always angry. When I'm not angry at the kids at school, I'm angry at my family, and I think I always will be. I'm like this even when I sleep now and it's so hard to control myself. I can't even tell if this is a dream or not right now.

"Do you need to use an adult diaper?" I ask mockingly with a fake look of concern. "Mommy keeps them for when she gets old and ugly."

"Kid put the gun down!" He tries to say calmly, but it sounds a bit too high pitched. I laugh louder, he sounds like a girl! "If you shoot that gun I'll kill your sister and you'll wake up your parents."

I don't want to put the gun down, he'll just hurt sissy if I put it down anyway. I remember what he did to her the last time! I refuse to trust him! Maybe if I shoot this he'll leave us alone forever. He'll be too scared to come back.

"Don't be scared, fatso, beebee guns don't hurt." I say darkly, then I aim towards his head and I inch my fingers towards the trigger. "You won't touch my sister ever again."

The guy glares at me in response. "That's a real gun." He sneers at me, and I glare right back at him. I look at the beebee gun, it does sort of look like the one he tried to shoot me with before. I could've gotten really hurt if he hadn't missed back then. I shake my head, he's just trying to scare me. It has a weird, black long thing attached to the barrel of it anyway, real guns don't look like that.

"Look kid, I'm just trying to find something that your mommy took from my cousin, Chase. It's not anything big, it's just a silver ring with the letters CS engraved on it."

That's Mommy's ring, not his! Mommy said she took it from a bad guy and she wears it to remember how she trusted him and he betrayed her.

"You mean the bad guy necklace?" I ask, but already know the answer. Mommy loves that necklace! I'm not giving it to him, it's Mommy's favorite and I wouldn't be able to give it to him even if I wanted to. Mommy leaves the necklace in a secret place and no one is allowed to touch it. I pull the trigger.

The man collapses to the ground, blood pouring out of his body. He doesn't move, he doesn't get up, his eyes are blurry like a fishes and his chest isn't moving up or down. The gun is real, it isn't a bee-bee gun. I don't know what to do so I just sit there and stare at his dead body.

I'm terrified, but I don't scream. No one wakes us and no one comes running. It wasn't loud, the thingy on the barrel is called a silencer, I think. My eyes are wide as I watch my hardwood floor flood with blood and I cry silently as I watch. I can't scream, I forget how.

If I killed someone, mommy would be very mad at me. Daddy is going to hate me. Am I going to be locked up in jail with all the rest of the bad guys?

I see black shoes walk in near my closet, they start to head towards me, but I don't run. They grab me, I don't struggle. They put a cold scratchy cloth on my mouth, I breathe in.

"Sorry Mommy," I mumble and then everything goes dark.

The scene changes rapidly and my sister is lying in a casket. I'm walking around the room and my family is crying as some priest invites my mom to stand up at the podium. She talks about how sweet and shy Lissa was. She talks about her in the past tense as if Lissa isn't alive.

Tears fall down my face and I shake my head as it dawns on me that this is a funeral. I run towards the casket and I see my twin's face but she isn't looking at me, her eyes are frozen shut forever. I sob as I realize that I wasn't able to save her in time. She's dead… I couldn't help her. The man kidnapped her despite all of my best efforts and mom and dad didn't come in time to rescue us. While my older siblings were fast asleep, even mom and dad, Lissa and I were struggling to keep ourselves alive. I was too weak to do anything to help at all.

I grab onto Lissa's hand and the freezing temperature of her lifeless hand has me struggling to breathe in pure terror. Just why did it end up like this? Am I really that useless?

"Lissa…" I choke out her name like it's food lodged in my throat. "Please, I need you."

Despite all my best efforts she doesn't respond. Why did the only person who understood me best in this world have to leave me like this? I needed her and now I'm left broken and alone.

Chapter 15

I WAKE UP IN A ROOM THAT I'VE EXAMINED TO BE THE NURSES OFFICE, my back is pressed against something hard and comfortable and arms are wrapped around my waist. Am I cuddling with someone? I can't be. I try to move, try to escape the arms surrounding me, but I can't.

The person who's trapped me has strong, muscular arms and a hard body. They smell like the saltwater in the ocean, I remember going on vacation to the beach in Florida. I remember the smell of the ocean, and this alluring scent is it.

Turning around, I gasp, Austen even looks troubled in his sleep, his eyebrows are furrowed and he's breaking into a sweat. He holds me closer to his chest, and I can't help but look at his full lips.

"Sorry Mommy," he whispers so softly I almost don't hear it. He looks so pained and tortured, my heart clenches at the sight of his mangled voice and I close my eyes shut. I try to move but he holds me even closer to him. "Sel, don't leave me." He croaks, and I open my eyes to see that he's staring directly at me.

"I'm right here Aus, I'm here," I kiss his cheek and look into his soft brown eyes. "I'm not gonna leave you, Aus." I say softly, trying to reassure not only him, but me.

He sighs and sits up, a mixture of confusingly sad emotions flashing in his eyes.

"Aus, huh? That's new." I laugh nervously, a blush spreading across my face.

"Sorry, do you not like it?"

"It's cute," he says with a small smile adorning his face. "Sort of like you."

His booming laughter makes me relax a bit, but I'm still curious. What was he dreaming about? Whatever this was, it seemed more terrifying than a nightmare. I've never seen Austen scared before in my life, yet this had him whimpering for his mom in fear.

"That must've been one terrifying dream though. Do you mind if I ask what it was about?" I ask breathlessly, my concern for him leaking out my voice like a running tap. I know that I'm running on dangerous territory; and I know that I'm not ready to tell him any of the things that have been going on with me, but I want to know.

His dark brown eyes harden and he refuses to look at me. His shoulders tense up like he has the weight of the world on them; and when he finally looks at me, I freeze.

Those broken looking eyes get to me, they wrap themselves around my heart and squeeze mockingly. Those eyes make me feel things that I haven't ever felt before in my entire life.

"I can't tell you," he says quietly and looks at me one last time, before standing up and leaving the room.

I follow him out of the room, watching how he moves slowly, sleepily, droopily, and I frown. What kind of dream could've made Austen so exhausted and sad? What kind of dream could make him look so ashamed of who he is? What is haunting him?

"Aus, please tell me!" I say pleadingly, putting my hand on his shoulder. "Please."

He turns to look at me, smoldering brown eyes filled with anguish and unshed tears.

"Little Sel, I haven't even told Lissa that I have these dreams occasionally, I really can't."

I glare at him because I want him to tell me. It hurts because I trust him and I want to know more about him. I want him to open up to me so I can open up to him. And more importantly, I scowl at him because I know I shouldn't want any of those things.

"I trust you more than I should for God knows what reason. I like you even though I know I damn well shouldn't, and seeing you like this is breaking my damn heart! I know it hurts, trust me I do, and I know that I shouldn't even be asking you this, but I don't know what else to do. We're in the same boat, Aus. I have these feelings for you, and I don't know how to explain them, but they're there, and they're making me scared. They're making me selfish. Please, tell me..."

His adam's apple bobs and his eyebrows furrow. He coughs a little bit and his eyes are getting glassy with every second that goes by.

"I don't want to hurt you, Sel." He says quietly, and I can feel my heart beating so fast in my chest. The sound of his voice makes me break apart. It sounded so broken and hoarse.

"If I could tell you, I would. The problem is the minute I open my mouth, you'll run in the opposite direction. I'm not someone that you should be trying so hard to understand. I'm a monster. I wish I could tell you, but the reality in this situation is that I can't. No matter what I tell you or don't tell you, you'll end up running away from me scared. You don't know the part of me that people gossip about. I've never yelled at you or fought with you the way that I do with other people. I've never been mean or cruel to you. The entire time we've been getting to know each other, you've seen the best sides of me and let's be real... you didn't like those parts of me either."

His eyes have gone hard and a slow smirk spreads across his face, all signs of tears and sadness have just vanished. He looks me dead in the eye, a malicious look on his face. It's as if he didn't cuddle up with me in the nurse's office, or beg me to stay with him. It's like he completely forgot all of the feelings, I know that he has, towards me.

"And if I have to introduce you to that monster so that it won't hurt as much when you go, I will. That's just who I am."

I glare at him one last time before the final bell rings and I start walking to Xavier's car, fuming at Austen's choice. The first day that we talked, he was a little annoying but he was kind, maybe that was only because he wanted something but still... Sure, he was arrogant, but that's a part of his charm. Then we started talking in English class more and he helped me home, twice. Now, he's choosing to just forget how much we clicked, He's willing to forget how much we have in common. He's deciding to forget our chemistry, our bond.

When I get home, as I wait for my mom I pull out my laptop and answer questions from my blog, when I get to one that makes my heart beat loudly in my chest. I shiver as I read it. The username might be anonymous, but I know exactly who sent it.

I hate that I'm burdened with this, but I can't change it. I'm stuck. I think I just lost Ms. Perfect, and I want her to know that I hate it as much as she does.

-ANONYMOUS

Chapter 16

AUSTEN'S POV

I WATCH HER AS SHE STORMS INTO SOME RANDOM DUDE'S CAR, AGAIN. I watch as the car starts. I watch as she leaves me.

My heart drops into my stomach and I feel like crying. As I try to swallow the lump in my throat, I try to forget the image of Lissa's cold lifeless body looked in the casket, something that could've been prevented if not for my incompetence. It was just a dream, I try to remind myself. I try to forget my own cruelty.

If I weren't so messed up, I could've told her everything about me. I would've spilt every secret I had. I would've wrapped my heart in a box and given it to her. Hell, technically, my heart belongs to her, I'm just being stubborn and refusing to hand it over despite her name that's clearly engraved on the wood of the box that holds it.

We could've been good together — in an alternate universe where I'm not crazy, sad, and broken. I could've taken her on a proper date, I could've taken her out to eat at a fancy restaurant. I could've made her laugh and smile all night long. I could've escorted her to her doorstep when it was time for her to go home, smiling the whole time like some kind of drunken fool, and then I could've kissed her.

I could've made her proud to date a sweet guy like me. She wouldn't have to warn anyone about all of my little triggers. If I met her parents she wouldn't have to tell her mom something like: "Hey mom, guess what? You can't stare at my boyfriend for too long cause' he'll black out and probably punch something," or "Hey mom, this is my boyfriend, Austen, he's been in a lot of fights and has terrible anger issues, but he's awesome because… he can be sweet sometimes despite the shouting and craziness… Actually you're right he doesn't deserve me. I'll break up with him tomorrow, don't worry."

Because I am that messed up and if I tell her all my secrets then she'll not only run away as fast as she can, she'll never want to associate with me again. If we ever got together now, I wouldn't just ruin her, she'd ruin me and I wouldn't be able to recover from all of that pain. She's got that kind of a hold on my heart. I don't think I can handle the pain I'll feel when she finally realizes I'm too broken.

The people around the school parking lot stare at me curiously, and I start to get uncomfortable. As more and more people stare, my blood begins to boil. Every stare reminds me that I'm a little piece of shit, I'm nothing, I'm not worthy of love, and the pure part of me that used to exist when I was little has been gone for a long ass time.

A scream rips through my throat and my vision goes black.

"Stop fucking staring at me!" I hear myself shout, my fists clenching so hard it's painful. I feel a hand touch my arm and I yank it off.

"Get the fuck off of me!" I growl loudly.

"Austen, dude it's me. Calm down."

I punch whoever the hell has just tried to touch me. And when my vision finally returns to me, I see Corbin doubled over, his hands on his stomach.

"I'm sorry Corbin, I didn't know it was you." I try to help him up off the ground and when he glares at me, I sigh. "I'm really sorry."

"It's fine, I was just trying to help you man. I know how you are."

Corbin is my best friend, my confidante. When other people have looked at me and judged me, he didn't. This guy recognizes that I have my anger issues, and he tries to help me. He's the only guy I've ever even considered telling about the nonstop dreams that I get. The dreams where I'm murdering the person who tried to take Lissa. The dreams where I only feel remorse after the guy's dead. At first, he wanted me to tell him about my past, and one day I almost did but he stopped me because he knew that I clearly wasn't ready. I'm glad I have a friend like him in my life. No one else would understand. He might be a chill dude but he's had a rough life too.

He told me about how his mom was arrested when he was around seven and how he lives with his dad. Mr. Jackson was always pretty buff, he never really spoke to me and I was kind of scared of him. One day I was at Corbin's house and Corbin and I were playing Shrek on his game cube when Mr. Jackson started shouting. I remember watching Corbin shake and him telling me I should leave. To this day, he still hasn't tried to explain it. I haven't asked him about it either. We have a sort of silent agreement that until we're both ready we won't tell each other all of the shit going on in our lives.

"It's okay man, are you ready to chill? Not at mine today, though, Dad's home."

"That's cool, but Lissa's gonna be home. Try not to drool all over her," I chuckle slightly when I see how uncomfortable he looks. "Come on dude, I know you like her."

He weaves his hand through his hair and sighs. When he looks at me he doesn't seem uncomfortable anymore, just sad.

"It doesn't matter, she barely thinks of me as a friend, and she likes that asshole Jake."

We both start walking to my car, and when we drive off, we sit in silence. We both think about the girls in our life that we know we can't be with.

When we get to my house I'm surprised to see Dad's car in the driveway. He's usually busy working in the family business, Hendrik's Place, it's a huge car retailer around our house and so we're pretty well off. If he's not there he's waiting for mom to get off work at Hamilton's Ring. She owns the place so she's usually spending a lot of time there too. My parents are just busy people. Since the other three idiots she raised moved out, Mom's been spending time working on her gym. I wish I could see mom more often but it is what it is. Kaden's probably gonna end up taking over dad's business and Kale's probably going to end up taking over mom's. Me, Lissa, and Angel, are trying to find other ways to make money in our future. The thought just stresses me out though.

So why is the old man here? Never mind, I probably did something.

Corbin and I get out of the car and when we get inside, Dad is watching TV with my depressed looking brother, Kale, and some random scrawny blonde guy.

"Mr. Hendrickson, what did Kale look like when he was younger? Did he always look like an adorable sad puppy?"

Kale has always been reserved and quiet, but this guy next to him somehow got Kale to actually defend himself.

"Will you kindly shut up? I don't look like a puppy."

Corbin looked at me and we both grinned, whoever this kid was got my brother to stop acting like a depressed German Shepherd.

"You might not have looked like one, but you sure as hell acted like it." I said loudly, making both the skinny blonde guy and Kale jump up.

"I don't know you, but if you want stories about this idiot, I'm your guy." I walk over to the sofa with Corbin and we sit down across from them. I would never miss an opportunity to completely embarrass *any* of my older brothers.

"Well, one day, when Kale and I were at this party..."

Chapter 17

Maybe it's the cold atmosphere that I'm being forced to adjust to when I first get into Xavier's car, but I wish I didn't walk away from Austen. I was being very hypocritical, he's not my boyfriend and even if he was, I wouldn't be able to be very honest with him either.

As I look out the window, trees blur past me and reform their shape. Usually, I'd take comfort in watching the dark green and brown blobs, but I can't seem to find comfort in anything lately. Everything that I could have ever wanted in life seems to pop into view and then when I go to grab it, it's snatched out of my reach and I'm left desperately trying to reach it. Lately, it's seemed as if somebody is just trying to taunt me.

I've never been so tired in my life, but I'm scared to fall asleep in his car. Xavier is capable of anything and everything, he's someone to be wary of and I recognize that. The fact that my dad has been pushing this to happen, is even worse.

When we arrive at my dad's place, I open the ugly brown car doors fervently and rush out of the car.

"Seline, your father wants you to meet him in his study." Xavier says assertively, and I sigh. Nothing I ever do will allow me to have a moment of peace from these two people. With them in my life, I'll never be happy.

Walking through the beige colored corridors and brown wooden floors, I reach my fathers office and I look at the white door. I'm tired, I'm so damn tired. I don't want to sort through files. I want to sleep. I want to dream. I want to do normal teenage girl things. I want to be a teenager, for once. I can't endanger anyone's lives doing what he asks me to do, and I definitely cannot sit down at a desk and put away his folders that are stacked full with all of his criminal activity.

I knock on my father's office door and before he can invite me in, I slam the door open and walk in. My dad's eyebrows arch in condescending confusion. He hasn't seen anybody disrespect him like this in a while, but I'm a teenager and I know how to throw a temper tantrum. I'm just so done with this man's crap, it's not even funny.

Crossing my arms, I glare at the man who abandoned me. He might not have left us because he wanted to, but in the end, he enjoys his life here and he wouldn't leave it for us. He relishes in all of the respect and glory. Since he started forcing me to come here, I've begun to notice certain things: he'll smirk when people comply with him. He laughs when people fear him. He probably feels like a king.

My dad justifies the position he's in by saying he loves his family and I even believed that maybe he did for a little while there but now? Nope. He doesn't love me at all. He believes, with all his heart, that he's only doing all of this for Mom and I. However, if there was an opportunity for him to leave the Mists, without him or any of our family being hurt, he wouldn't take it. I know he wouldn't.

Dad would stay here and he would continue to get normal people involved in drugs and sex trafficking. He would continue to make people indebted to him. He would continue to kill people without flinching, and he would continue to make people cover up his tracks.

The man in front of me will never change the way he is, and that's okay. It's time for me to move on. It's time for me to defend myself and keep him from having such a huge impact on my life. If I want my life to be better, I need to remove him from the equation. I need to finally stand up for myself. If I want my life to get better, I need to stop letting him control me. That talk with Austen cleared up a lot of things for me. He's controlled by his demons and so he feels as if he can't share them with anybody. Yet I wanted to help him get through them so badly. If he were to have just told me what he was thinking or feeling then maybe we'd be able to work things out together. He didn't though. Just like me, he's scared that I'll be hurt one day. If I continue to let this man control me, I'll never be able to trust anybody. I'll never be able to live my life.

"I'm not helping you anymore, Dad." My voice is clear, loud, and assertive. Nothing is going to get in my way anymore. My dad is not going to hold this power over me.

"Is that so?" He asks with a chuckle, folding his hands together and placing them down on his work. "If I remember clearly, you're not the one who gets to choose when you stop working for me. I'm still the one with the power here. I can kill your boyfriend. I know where he lives. It won't take a long time."

I smirk at him this time, maybe he thinks he has that power right now, but after I'm done talking, he won't.

"You let me touch your computer, you let me hold records in my hands that the police would consider evidence. You're an idiot. You have no idea what I'm capable of. You aren't going to touch Austen, and neither is anyone from your gang because if you do, I'm going to the authorities with everything."

I smile wickedly, I'm not sure if the things that I sent to my computer would be enough to get daddy dearest sent to jail. I'm not even sure if I want him in jail, but it's worth a try.

"Oh, and, try and come to my house to erase the records and I'll send them anyway. Let's just say, I have more than one copy."

He jumps out of his seat and walks towards me with a dangerous glint in his eyes. My dad seethes as he walks towards me and he laughs darkly.

"You wouldn't tell anybody anything, you wouldn't dare. I'm your dad and you love me."

I look him dead in the eyes and walk a little bit closer to him, the tension in the room is so thick it rivals smoke.

"You left me for this life, Dad. When you did it, you say it was for a good cause, but nothing can justify leaving my mother to suffer through that horrible depression. Nothing can justify killing people for sport and nothing can justify all of the horrible things that you've done. The reason that you've stayed so long without contacting us wasn't because you were trying to keep us safe. It was because you were embarrassed by how much you enjoy this life and how much you crave it. You brought me here because the guys in your gang are scared that I'll squeal, right? Well then here's the solution to the problem, let me go. If you don't let me go, I'll snitch. I don't want to be a part of your illegal lifestyle. I don't want to see you kill and murder people, because I think it's wrong. I don't want to live in this cage. The only way that I'm not going to tell the world that you're a criminal, is if you let me go."

Dad growls angrily and rears his hand back to slap me, I don't even flinch when I feel the harsh sting of his rough palm coming into contact with my face. I don't scream or cry, I just hold my cheek in my hand.

He looks at me again but this time with sad eyes and when he opens his mouth to speak, I turn my back on him. I walk towards the door and I walk out of that dreadful office with no regrets.

I hear footsteps behind me, but I don't bother to turn around, I keep marching towards the room with the hidden tunnel inside it. Instead of just sitting down and letting things happen, for once, I'm not taking any risks.

It's time for me to tell Austen everything.

Chapter 18

AUSTEN'S POV

"**K**ALE WAS SIXTEEN, AND I HAD JUST TURNED FOURTEEN. KADEN wanted to go to this party and Kale didn't really want to go, but because Kaden asked him to, he decided to go. Kale ended up taking me to the party too, even though I just wanted to sleep, because he was scared Kaden would ditch him. Which he did, no surprise there. Kaden's a prick.

Every single time a girl would walk up to Kale and try to talk to him, he would ignore them. I mean I knew he was gay, but he could've at least talked to them instead of ignoring them.

Guys came up and tried to flirt with him too, and all he would do is blush like a damn tomato.

He didn't drink a damn thing the whole night while I got my first taste of alcohol. When Kale finally had enough of his moping around, he decided to drag me away from my fun and take me home. I was fourteen years old and this girl's been eyeing me all night, I was so sure I could've lost my virginity then and there, your boyfriend has terrible timing. If I wasn't drunk, I would've beat his ass.``

Corbin starts laughing beside me, and I smile.

"Is that the only thing you care about?" He asks with a chuckle. No. I care about so much more then sex and alcohol. I think I've had sex like twice, and both times I regretted it, both times I was drunk. As for alcohol and parties, I rarely drink and parties aren't really my scene. Parties require eye contact and bodies brushing up against random strangers, I'm not very fond of the idea. Either way, I smirk and nod my head.

Kale blushes, obviously embarrassed by me. The blonde-headed dude had put his hand over his mouth a while back, but now he's just chuckling loudly.

Dad and I smirk at Kale and I smile when Kale fixes his pointed glare on Dad too.

"Why is that story so amusing to you guys? It's perfectly normal for a teenager to not find parties entertaining." He says, scoffing under his breath. "Just because I didn't, and still don't think, I should've drowned all of my brain cells and gotten laid at sixteen, which by the way is before I was even legal, doesn't mean I was acting like a puppy. It just means that I was and still am responsible and smart."

I raise my eyebrows at him mockingly and lean forward, folding my hands together on my knees.

"No, but the fact that you were willing to even go to the party just to hang out with your lame ass twin, who didn't care enough about you to actually hang with you, is evidence enough. You knew you wouldn't like the party, but you still came, because you followed Kaden everywhere. Just. Like. A. Damn. Puppy."

Kale scoffs, again, and chuckles mockingly with a nod. He grabs his boyfriend's hand and breathes in and out with closed eyes. My smirk grows as shaggy, what I've named Kale's boyfriend, smiles softly. I never thought I'd see the day when Kale would find someone for him.

"Remember the time when Kaden convinced Kale to shave off all of your hair?" Corbin asks, chuckling. "You weren't even mad at him!"

I smile evilly at Kale as he slumps into the couch.

"Yeah, how could I ever forget that? He was nice enough to make it look good, and girls would stare at me for hours at school. It made life a bit easier at school for a while, people were looking at me differently. They weren't as scared. Didn't stop me from replacing Kaden and Kale's soap with paint, though, their skin was blue for like three days."

Corbin and I laugh really hard, we're practically cackling all the while, Kale, glares at us. But in all honesty it was his own fault he was blue for three days, if he would've just said no to Kaden and left me alone, none of that would've happened.

"Shaggy, your little Kale over here didn't have a mind of his own. He let Kaden walk all over him, just because he didn't like a little bit of conflict. Kaden always got away with everything because of my dearest older brother, and it was annoying as hell. Kaden got Kale to do whatever the hell he pleased. What pissed me off the most about Kale's puppy-like behavior, though, was when he would help Kaden prank my twin sister, Lissa. See, unlike him and Kaden, I protect my twin at all costs and I don't take advantage of her."

I try my damnedest not to look resentful towards Kale, but it starts to become so damn hard. I never liked looking back at our history because I know what actually went on. Behind closed doors, our pranks and arguments were more than just little sibling squabbles, we had and still do have, a rivalry. All I wanted to do was embarrass my asshole brother in-front of his boyfriend. I didn't want to show him how much I actually resent my brother, but the look on both of their faces and the look on Dad and Corbin's faces, shows that I have in fact failed.

Kale starts nervously biting on his fingernails and he gives me this sad look. Shaggy glares at me and Corbin nudges me with his elbow. My dad sighs and pinches the bridge of his nose.

"Sorry I didn't mean to snap at you guys." Dad nods his head as if he understands something I don't and I clench my fists in my lap. Looking at the three sad and confused faces, staring up at me like I murdered their puppy, I begin to feel overwhelmed. Standing up, I walk over to my room with slumped shoulders. I'm starting to feel so sick and tired of how familiar the feeling of guilt is to me.

I slam my bedroom door shut behind me and throw myself onto my bed. An agitated groan burst through my lips, I should know better by now. Why can't I keep my damned mouth shut!? Shouting loudly at nothing in particular, I punch my pillow. This is why I hate it when my stupid older siblings come home from college; they all bring out the worst in me. I get on my phone and send a quick comment on Sel's blog, hoping that maybe she'll see it. I know that it's anonymous and she probably won't know it's me, but I just need to express to her how I feel.

Tap, tap, tap. I hear three sharp knocks coming from my bedroom door. Tap, tap, tap. There it is again, this time I freeze. For a split second, I wonder if dad decided to come up here and yell at me for embarrassing Kale the way I did. It was either him or Corbin. I did end up just leaving him in the living room with them, he's probably not too happy. Two more sharp knocks sound, and I find myself walking to my door. Sighing at my own stupidity as I go to open the door. I'm obviously not in the right mood to be scolded but I kind of deserve it anyway. I freeze at the door knob and sigh. I twist the door knob ready for the chaos that will bring when I do.

No words can explain how utterly confused I am by who I see.

Chapter 19

"WHAT THE FUCK ARE YOU DOING HERE!?" AUSTEN ASKS WITH wide eyes. He drags me inside of his room, looking completely bewildered and… angry? Why's he so angry to see me at his place? He pushes me up against the wall of his small closet. The hanger for a black long sleeve shirt hits my arm lightly, and I bite down on my tongue.

"How'd you even know where I live?" He asks me, his eyes glaring into my own, and I can't look away. His sharp and angular face is a breath away from my own. My eyes open wide as I realize why he's so confused. He's never taken me to his house and it's not like I could get that information from school. I just randomly showed up at his place despite the fact that I shouldn't even know where he lives. I got this information from my dad too… This looks awful.

"Let me explain, please, I know how bad this looks, but I can explain." I say to him, my eyes softening as I look up at him. He lets go of my forearms and then scratches his head with a weird look on his face. He backs away from me a little bit and I turn around to close the closet door. He shouldn't leave it open anyways.

Austen walks towards his bed and I stare at him for a minute, just standing next to the closet. I look around and tug at my bottom lip, deciding to follow him. He plops down onto his bed, propping his head up onto a pillow so he can look in my direction. Pacing back and forth in front of Austen's bed, I comb my fingers through my hair.

"Explain." He says, his gaze cold and expectant.

"Okay, but it's a long story and it might take a while to get to the point," I murmur with a sigh. "My dad left my mom when I was seven. It traumatized my mom, and so, for a while, I was taking care of her. She slept all day and cried all night, and when I woke up in the mornings, I would cry while I got myself ready for school. All I understood was that my mom was sad and lonely and my dad was nowhere to be seen, and I had no friends to comfort me either."

Austen sits up on the bed and raises an eyebrow at me. His shirt rides up a little bit, and I try to ignore how hot he looks just sitting on his bed like that.

"I used to draw pictures of my dad and tape them on my wall. I remember one day I was so confused and just wanted to know where he was and so I just wanted to find out where he was, not only for me but for my mom as well. After I found out he was the boss of a gang called the Mists, I remember tearing every single one of them up. For weeks, I would cry myself to sleep because I felt so betrayed. We used to just sit down on the old black couch in the living room and watch movies. We would laugh until we cried while watching mostly Disney movies, laughing at the princesses and princes because we thought they were stupid. Dad used to say 'Baby, you're gonna grow up to be just like me.' He thought I would be adventurous, carefree, and happy. Well, he was wrong. I'm lonely, Austen, so freaking lonely." Austen's gaze softens, he frowns, and he scoots towards the edge of his bed. I cough awkwardly. "He knew me better than I knew myself and then he left me so that he could lead a stupid gang. I felt lost, like he never even cared about me. It felt like he stabbed me in the heart."

Austen grabs my hand and squeezes it, smiling at me, trying to get me to continue.

"After he left us, I couldn't talk to anyone about anything. My dad was my best and only friend and when he left, I had no one. I guess when you have no one, you observe other people more closely. You can watch how different people react to certain body languages and see how people express how they feel towards others, without saying a word. My favorite thing to see was love, I guess because I wanted love so much. Romantic love was the kind I was the most curious about. I would walk to the park, after my mom cried herself to sleep, and I would just watch as couples had their morning jogs.

"I watched when elderly couples walked by the park hand in hand. I watched when teenagers would sit at the benches and flirt with one another. My favorite movies were romantic and my favorite books were romantic. I was obsessed with all things romance. When I got older, I started staying at the park later, so I could observe more people's relationships. I knew it was intrusive, but I thought of it as studying, I was learning things. I've seen abusive relationships, unhealthy relationships, and quick relationships. I learned to understand them, because I could understand the people inside them.

"Eventually, I got to a point where I could offer advice to people. I could offer advice to people who were dealing with abusive and unhealthy relationships, and I tried to help. I researched things online, just to make sure that my methods were valid. I worked hard, because I realized just how hard it is for a person to get out of these relationships. I worked hard, because I wanted to help people. But I was alone in my observations, no one was going to benefit off of the things that I've noticed. No one wanted me, so it was ridiculous to keep the information to myself anyway. I tried to build my own blog. I researched millions of ways to make it successful, and eventually I did it. Cupid's Soldier became a hit, people came to me for relationship advice, and I like to believe I help them. I know none of this answered any of your questions, but this is just the beginning. You're the only person I trust, and I just want to show you who I am." I chuckle lightly. "You're literally the only person that I can talk to."

Austen watches me, his brown eyes intense and heated. Without taking his eyes off of me, he walks off the bed, the bed creaks with every stride of his long legs. He lands right in front of me, gazing into my eyes like a predator. He moves to grab my hand and I sit down in front of him on the bed. My eyes locked onto his and I felt comforted by the sweetness in his chocolate brown eyes.

A soft looking piece of hair falls on his face, I resist the urge to brush it away. Wanting to just touch his face, my fingers twitch at my sides.

"Sel, why are you here?" He whispers, looking into my eyes. My lips part and I gasp when he pulls me closer. Our noses are touching and I keep glancing at his very familiar lips.

"I would need to explain the rest of the story for you to understand." Looking up at him, I bite my lip and swallow. "It's a bit long, so bear with me." He just nods his head, not noticing his brown hair tickling my forehead, I smile.

"I'll start with when I figured out he was a gang leader."

"When I was twelve, I was tired of feeling helpless, so I started looking for him. At first, I just asked around the neighborhood, but no one would talk. After that, I tried logging into his old email address, but he changed the password. So I started looking through police reports online. It was my last hope. I remember going on the website and typing my dad's last name. I found an article on my grandpa, it gave me a source of clarity. It said my grandpa, Craw, was speculated to be a vital member in a gang called the Mists and that he was found shot and dead in a forest." Austen stiffens. "Before my Uncle Stefan died, overdosing on Heroin, two weeks after my father disappeared, he was suspected to be in that very same gang. I'm a smart girl, so I put two and two together. If gang leaders get passed on through blood and his family is dead, then my dad must've been a part of it. At first, it was all just speculation because the police hadn't arrested my dad or any of my family yet. Until I hacked into his email and found the confirmation myself. It took me a while but I finally figured out his password.

I thought that note on my locker was from my dad, especially since the colors were his gang colors. But, it was from my uncle, his half brother. I was so scared, Aus." My voice breaks and a tear falls down my face, Austen brushes it away and smiles.

"Sel, it's okay. Finish what you were saying." The tenderness in his voice surprises me, but I do what he says.

"He wanted an excuse to see me, around the time that you kissed me, so he got my uncle to kidnap me. He took me, while I was on my way to school he just drugged me and took me. He locked me up in a cold cellar with a springy uncomfortable mattress and told me that I needed to work for him. He threatened you, Aus, he said that if I told the police or anyone, he'd hurt you. At first I did everything he said, I helped him sort documents and files and I helped him with calls. I was like his little secretary. But I wanted it to stop. I came to warn you that I threatened him and I told him that if he ever tries to put his hands on you or anyone else that I care about that I'm going to leak his files to the police. I'm tired of being lonely, Aus, for the first time in my life I'm being selfish. I want to take what I want without permission. And

I want you." My words start coming out rushed as he trails his hands that were holding mine to my waist. He grabs the back of my neck with his other hand and he slams his lips on mine. I moan into the kiss. My eyes flutter shut and I surrender to the electric feeling of his lips moving with mine. Wrapping my arms around his neck, I run my fingers through his perfect soft brown hair. His hands move to hold my cheeks and I moan as I feel the unfamiliar sting of tenderness behind his touch. My heart beats a rhythm to a song about us, a song that makes me forget everything but him. He pulls away from me, and we stare at each other. His full lips are now red and puffy; his eyes are dilated, his hair is all over the place, and a ghost of a smile is appearing on his face. I can't keep my eyes off of him.

"You don't need to be alone anymore, Sel."

He grabs my hand and leads me towards his bed. We sit, our legs crossed and our knees touching. Staring at each other in silence for what feels like eternity, until Austen breaks the silence.

"Now that you've spilled your guts, it's my turn."

Chapter 20

I'M NOT NERVOUS, BUT HE SEEMS TO BE. HIS GORGEOUS BROWN eyes are wide, he's tearing at his bottom lip with his teeth, and he keeps running his fingers through his hair. I grab the hand he has laying next to my leg, and I massage it with my thumb. When he looks up at me, I smile, and when his eyes seem to grow more intense and determined, I bite my lip. The uncomfortable feeling of want, burns at my core.

"Lissa, doesn't even know about all of this yet. She knows about a little chunk of it, but I can't tell her the rest. I'm too scared to."

"She's your twin, you protect her and love her. I have no doubt in my mind that she would do the same for you."

He gives me a weird look, a look that seems to insinuate that I have no idea what I'm talking about. Maybe he's right, but I have taken care of my mom since I was seven. When things got bad, I was always by her side. We struggled through a lot of things, but because we love each other, we persevered. He's underestimating the love his sister must have for him.

Raising my hands in surrender, I smile.

"Go ahead." I say, nodding my head at him expectantly. "You want to know why I have all those bad dreams, right?" I nod my head again, and he smiles nervously.

"When I was six years old, Lissa almost got kidnapped and I almost got shot. It was really late at night and everyone was in their beds. Lissa was hiding underneath hers. I guess she heard him coming from the closet and thought he was a monster or something, but she was hiding. I yelled for my mom and dad and they came running up the stairs, that's when he grabbed her. I grabbed a bat from my closet and I hit him in his knee with it so that he'd let her go and then when my mom and dad finally got in the room he shot at me. Thankfully, he missed, but I could've died. " I gulp. The thought of him dying almost at that young age is terrifying. "My parents called the ambulance because I'd fainted and they couldn't get me to wake up. Apparently the doctor's were afraid that I could've gone deaf too. I'm lucky to be alive and that I can still hear right now. After that I was always sort of a mean kid. The doctors say that my anger issues probably come from my mom, they're genetic. But, I never really felt all of that anger until the helplessness from that day. Little Sel, I never want to feel like that again."

I look at him, really look at him, and lift my finger up to bite my nail. That was obviously the part, Alissa, knew about. If it's already pretty horrible, just how bad does his past get?

"In elementary school, I was a bully. I was horrible. If someone wanted to get on the slide on the playground, I forced them to literally bow down to me. It made me feel more in control, I guess. I remember that if a boy tried to get on the slide without bowing, I would fight them. I would get so furious if anybody tried to break my rules. I would yell at girls and fight boys. I would suck up to teachers and get their sympathy, and for the longest time, I felt like a king."

I watch the smirk on his face, and instead of feeling disgusted, I'm just sad. Yes, he did terrible things. The thing is though, he was a kid. He was a troubled, scarred, child, who needed help and because he didn't get it he got into trouble.

"Lissa always got me out of trouble. She was always helping me and bailing me out. But, she couldn't get me out of all of it. Eventually, I started having nightmares about Lissa dying. The dreams would always begin with me murdering the man who kidnapped Lissa and then it would end with Lissa dying because I couldn't keep her safe. Years passed and it began to get hard for me to sleep. My parents even started noticing that I wasn't sleeping at night and they took me to a psychiatrist.

I was diagnosed with Insomnia, Post Traumatic Stress Disorder, and Anger Issues. They worry about me still to this day but I didn't want to keep going to therapy so instead I take melatonin. I still have nightmares but they don't know that. They think that I've been getting better. I'm not. I'm struggling just to make it in this life. I lash out at everyone and I always think that I'm being looked down upon. I'm always paranoid. I can't trust anyone. I don't know… I probably should still be in therapy but I really don't want to talk about my issues. I don't want to remember if I don't have to. It's normal for children of well-off families to be at risk for kidnapping. It happens all the time in America. It's the ransom money that they're usually after. Thing is though, the man was looking for something. Sometimes I remember things that he said like he was looking for a ring with CS engraved onto it and other nonsense but I was too young to remember clearly what exactly it was. As long as we still have it, I have no doubt in my mind that he'll try again eventually and I'm honestly scared. If he does come back… I don't think I'll have the strength to just let him by. To let the police handle it. If he comes back, I'll end up being a murderer. That's the kind of thinking I'm capable of, little Sel. You're so bright and good, why'd you have to fall for someone so completely broken? "

My eyes are wide and they're watering as I look up at him. His eyes are almost as wide as my own and a tear has already run down his cheek. I put my hand on his face and brush it away with the pad of my thumb. Caressing the slight and sexy stubble on his jaw, I have no idea what to say to him so instead I kiss his closed eyelids. Afterwards, I kiss his cheek and then I kiss his other one. Just when I'm about to kiss his full lips I hear the creaking of a door.

He bites his bottom lip and he looks down at his legs.

"Austen?"

I gasp and Austen looks back up, his eyes wide and panic flashes through them. His whole face pales and he looks everywhere but his family. The woman who's standing next to Alissa, at the bedroom door, is gorgeous. She has a very fit body, her eyes are stunning brown, and her hair is shiny and thick.

"M-mom?" He stutters over his words. "Lissa?" He whispers, and I wrap my arms around him. Giving him one last kiss on his soft cheek, I look at the two girls, and smile.

"I should get going." I say, and start moving off Austen's bed.

"No. Please, stay. I think it would be easier for Austen, if we speak to him about this with you here." His mom says, her voice soft and lovely, even after hearing all of the emotional things her son went through.

Alissa smiles at me, and I find the strength to sit back down.

Chapter 21

"WHY DIDN'T YOU TELL US YOU WERE STILL HAVING NIGHTMARES, Austen? You can't just hide something like that." Mrs. Hendrickson says to Austen, her slim fingers pinching the bridge of her nose. Alissa is sitting on Austen's desk chair, in the corner of his room, one of her legs is crossed over the other, her elbows are resting on her knees, her hands covering her eyes, and I sympathize with her. I know how it feels to find out that someone you admire and inspire to be like has been hiding something from you. Especially when it's something that has something to do with you. She probably thinks that it's somehow her fault. too.

"I couldn't tell you guys, Mama. I can trust you guys with a lot of things, but if you guys thought that something was still wrong with me then you'd all be even more careful around me than you already are. I was a scared kid who bullied people and lashed out at other's but that doesn't mean that I was dumb. Lissa already blamed herself for what happened and if she saw that I wasn't healing she'd think my brokenness is her fault. Newsflash, Lissa, it isn't." I grab his hand again, looking straight in his direction. His angular jaw clenches, his brown eyes dart from his mom to Alissa, and he grips my hand.

Mrs. Hendrickson nods her head in understanding, she seems to ponder over the information for a couple of seconds, and then she smacks him upside his head. Austen yelps and Alissa muffles her laugh by covering her mouth with her hand.

"We will always love you, you stupid boy." He scrunches his nose up, and I giggle when he looks at me and sticks his tongue out. He's adorable. "We're family, we would've found a way to help you Austen, we would've protected you. You were a child, we were supposed to be protecting you, not the other way around. It would've been easier for us to help if you would have told us sooner, but thankfully, it's not too late. You're going back to therapy if I have to drag you there."

Mrs. Hendrikson glances at me and smiles, her familiar brown eyes light up. She taps her fingers on her full lips and smirks.

"Now, Seline, isn't it?" She asks, and I nod.

"Yes, Mrs. Hendrikson."

"Please, don't call me that," she says. "That was my mother in law's name." My eyebrows furrowed in confusion, then what should I call her? I don't know her first name, and even if I did I wouldn't call her by it, and I can't just come up with a name to call her.

"Just call me Lia or Ms. Lia." Her bright smile is back, but this time, it seems a bit forced. She walks closer to the bed, and puts her soft hand on my shoulder.

"It's good to meet the girl my son's so in love with." I glance at Austen from the corner of my eye. He shrugs and shakes his head at me. I dismiss the little pang of disappointment inside my chest. I don't think I'm in love with him yet, I have no right to be sad that he isn't in love with me. Ms. Lia glares at Austen and scowls.

"What did I say about lying? Tell the poor girl the truth."

Austen's cheeks turn into this adorable scarlet color, I resist the urge to reach out and pinch them, grinning at his cuteness.

"Mama, stop being ridiculous. This isn't any of your business."

"Shut up, Austen." She says, glaring at him. "He's never brought a girl home before. He would claim it was because girls were scared of him, which I assume is partly true, but I don't think he was very interested in dating either. Now look at you, Seline: you're inside of our house, you're getting him to open up, and he hasn't said a bad thing about you once. He loves you. I'm his mother, trust me, I know."

I laugh, my voice breaking in nervousness. Her determined gaze on me is confusing. What exactly is she gaining from telling me that he loves me? If he feels that way, shouldn't he tell me himself?

"We met each other around two months ago or so..." I trail off, unable to describe our relationship these past months. The time that we did spend together was either stressful, amazing, or some combination of the two. Every time that we weren't together, I never stopped missing him. "Austen, isn't in love with me Ms. Lia." My voice cracks into nothingness and the room becomes eerie and silent. I glance at Austen, and I know exactly what I feel: love. Our gazes lock onto one another's and I gulp, nothing is safe about how I feel, even though, as I look at him, I feel safe. His dark brown eyes burn into me, unknown emotions swirling inside of them. He squeezes my hand again, and I look away.

I lean towards him and kiss his cheek, lingering there for a little bit just to feel his skin against my lips. "I should probably leave now. It was nice meeting you, Ms. Lia, I'll see you at school Alissa." I jump off of the bed and I walk around Ms. Lia, to leave the room.

"Little Sel, wait!"

I start running down the oak stairs in desperation. Three men are sitting on couches in the cozy looking living room, and I try to run out of there unnoticed by them. The door is only a couple feet away from the couches, so it shouldn't be that hard. I run my fingers through my hair and my pulse races.

"Sel, wait up!" His voice alerts the three men of my presence. They all turn around to look at me and I gasp in astonishment. I didn't really take notice of the way he looked before when he opened the door but Mr.Hendrikson looks exactly like Austen, except his eyes are a bright blue. I thought Ms. Lia looked like Austen, and he does; he has her features, complexion, eye color, and disposition. The way that they hold themselves is basically the same. But Austen's father, he has his face shape, the intense stare, his jawline...

A hand grabs my wrist and twirls me around until I'm face to face with Austen. I'm staring into his eyes again, my heart is racing, and I can't breathe properly. My chest is pressed against his and his hand is holding mine against his chest. He leans down, his breath tickling my ear.

"I love you," he whispers into my ear.

I gasp and look up into his gorgeous brown eyes, and I grin. My fingers trail over his hard chest, to his slim neck, and then they run through his soft hair. I kiss him with vigor, slamming my lips onto his full ones, my heart flips inside of my chest. A cough breaks through the air, and I pull myself away from him.

"Can you please find another area in the house to make out with your girlfriend?" Austen's dad asks, and my cheeks warm.

"Can I leave now?" I ask, my fight or flight instincts kicking in.

"Actually, no, you've already met my mom and my twin; now, I would like you to meet the rest of my family. The guy pursing his lips like he doesn't know how to smile is my pain in the ass older brother and the blonde guy he's got his arms wrapped around is his boyfriend. You can just call him shaggy or blondie, that's what I do. I don't know his name just yet, it's irrelevant. And my dad's the old-looking guy on the loveseat."

I run my fingers through my disheveled hair, and gulp. I'm scared.

Chapter 22

"Austen, you know you're not allowed to do that shit in my house." His dad says, intimidating blue eyes pointing in my direction and thick black eyebrows raised. "And didn't you say that you and Austen were just friends, little lady?"

My cheeks flame in response to my embarrassment. He probably thinks that I'm some kind of stalker or that I'm one of Austen's flings. I'm not sure which one is the most embarrassing.

"U-um, yeah we're just friends I think… you'll have to ask him. I don't want to be here when he tells you. I've had enough drama for today." I stutter over my words like an idiot. Austen's dad probably thinks the worst of me, I made a terrible first impression. But I don't care, today was ridiculous. When I wasn't running away from my dad, I was spouting my life story to the guy I think I'm in love with. And when I wasn't spouting my life story, I was being told that Austen's in love with me. It's been an eventful and terrifying day. For a split second, I let myself believe that I love him. But I don't know what I feel towards Austen, I know I care about him. I know that I feel safe with him and I know that I want him. I know that I've never felt this way about someone in my entire life. I'm confused.

"Where did Corbin go?" Austen asks, looking around the living room for his friend.

"He just went to get something to eat from the kitchen." Austen's brother scoffs. "Do they not feed you guys at school or something? Does he not have food at home? He's been in and out of the kitchen since you left, about an hour ago."

Austen gaze shoots daggers at his brother. Corbin is someone that Austen will defend no matter what. I wish I had a friendship like that.

"Kale, shut up. His life at home isn't any of your business, and school lunch costs money."

Austen stomps into the kitchen, leaving me alone with these three strange men, who are staring at me.

"Are you his girlfriend, stalker, or fling?" Kale, I think that's his name, questions me. The blunt expression on his face makes me blush.

"I'm none of those things. At the moment, we're just friends." But the silent hope that we could grow into more than that, isn't buried or gone.

Kale raises a fluffy thick eyebrow at me in disbelief, and scoffs.

"Then why are you even here? And why were you two making out in the hallway and looking at each other like food?"

"I don't have an answer for that, sorry."

His dad smirks and stands up, he's tall, he's definitely passed six feet. He starts moving towards me with a small smile on his face. He looks at me and his eyes dance in realization.

"Kale, look at her, he's more like me than we thought." He crosses his arms and looks down at me with a pleased smile. Nodding his head at me, like I'm some type of inanimate portrait. I glare at him, but he doesn't seem to notice. "You're really smart, right? You get all A's on your report card every semester. You're nervous, probably scared out of your little mind, but you know you shouldn't be because you've been through worse. Much worse. I bet you're sassy and sarcastic too, he's got his old man's-"

"I. Am. A. Human. Being!" I say, raising my voice a little, all of his correct assumptions grating at my nerves. "I'm not a lab rat! You can't just assume things about me and then talk about me like I'm not standing here, right in front of you." I scoff, muttering to myself. "I can see where he gets his manners from too."

My face is flushed in anger, as I snap at him, but he isn't fazed by me at all. He seems to be even more amused than he was before. A small smirk is hanging off his face, and I gulp.

I just yelled at Austen's father, my eyes grow large as I realize what I've done.

"I'm so sorry." My voice starts shaking as I realize how rude I was. "I really shouldn't have yelled at you."

"Did you hear that, Kale? This girl's a keeper! She'll fit right in with the family. I'll bet you three thousand dollars that he's gonna end up marrying her!" He laughs, and smiles at me.

"It's okay, sweetheart. I didn't mind at all, if anyone was in the wrong it was me."

"I bet you he'll screw up, at least twice, before they get married." Kale adds, laughing along with his dad.

"I'm still here," I say motioning towards me. All three of them look towards me and smile.

"My name isn't blondie, by the way, and I'd appreciate it if you didn't call me that. Call me Jenson."

I smile awkwardly, waving at him.

"My name's Seline. Austen does have a lot to talk to you guys about though, just don't give him a hard time please. I know I'm not family and you barely know me, but this is important. He's told me that he's not that great at talking to family, and tonight he needs to say some things. Let him talk."

When Austen comes back with Corbin, I smile. Walking over to him, I kiss his cheek.

"Bye." I whisper in his ear, and he shivers. I smile and let my lips linger against his cheek for a couple of seconds, his heat enveloping me in warmth and comfort. He smiles at me, and I smile back, waving my hand at the rest of his family, I walk away from him.

Running out of the door, I close the door softly as I walk into the chili night air. Once I reach a park, I sit down on a bench and take my phone out of my pocket. Dialing a taxi service number, I hear footsteps behind me. When I turn around to see who's behind me, I gasp. The hair on the back of my neck rises as I see someone tall heading towards me.

I run, fast, away from the park bench. I stumble when I try to put my phone in my pocket, and I sprint harder. A hand circles around my waist, trying to lift me off the ground. I scream, my voice so loud and sharp, the rough grip on my waist tightens.

I kick and kick as I continue to struggle and try to wiggle away. My screams are loud enough to wake up the neighbors, but no one comes. The person tries to cover my mouth, but I bite their hand until a rush of bitter copper liquid burns my throat. Blood.

I scream louder and louder, until the person who is holding onto me punches me hard. I sob as the crack of his fist bruises my back.

"Help! Somebody! Help me!" I shout louder. The man holds my arms back, my back is in so much pain, I feel like I can't move. My legs don't kick anymore.

"Shut the fuck up!" A voice I recognize as my uncle's, shouts. He covers my mouth to muffle my screams, and I kick and flail. He doesn't let me go.

He grabs me and lifts me over his shoulders, I pound my fists on his back, and he grunts. I know that I'm in a lot of trouble when he throws me in the backseat of his car. Tears fall down my face, as he bends down and covers my eyes and mouth with some sort of cloth.

"Now, you're going to be quiet and listen to me. Whether you would like to believe it or not, this is for your own damn good."

Chapter 23

As the car continues to roll across the street, I continue to silently sob. I knew I needed to be scared around Xavier, but I didn't think that he'd ever try to hurt me physically.

"Do you remember when I would come over to visit your dad? I know I'm not your favorite person in the world, especially since you found out about the locker, but I still care about you."

I glare at him, my face stained with tears. My hands are tied with rope, my back. My feet are pressed together, bound. If my feet weren't tied, I would kick him. Someone who cares about you doesn't punch you. A person who genuinely has affection for you wouldn't tie and lock you up. If they loved me like they claim to they wouldn't even put me in situations like these. Which seems to be something that my dad and my uncle don't understand.

"Seline, I used to babysit you. Your dad never trusted our brother around you, you were too good and he had no soul, but he trusted me. I've called you something cruel, but I needed your attention. If you didn't understand the gang colors, I had to put a message you'd understand. I know that you're not a slut. Your dad asked me to get your attention, so I got a recruit in the school to help me out and told him that if he painted that message on your locker with our gang colors, I'll back him up. As for punching you, I'm sorry. I didn't do it to hurt you, I just needed you to come with me and you were drawing attention to yourself." I wiggle in my seat and wave my tied hands so he can see them. He shakes his head. "I'm not going to untie your hands, but I'll untie your mouth. I need you right here, right now. There were men circling Austen's house, ready to pounce. It might not be today or tomorrow, but they're watching and waiting for your dad's call. I love you. I swear to you that I do, baby girl. I'm going to park the car for a second. Please don't try anything hasty, I need your full cooperation for this to work." His calm and low voice echoes through the car. He stops the car in a McDonald's parking lot, leans towards me and unties the rope around my mouth. He watches me, his eyes serious and calm. He looks away, focuses back on the road, and speeds out of the small parking lot.

"What I'm about to tell you, is important and it's going to help us both. Your dad needs to be removed, he's a terrible leader. He's going to run this gang into the ground. At first, he was a good leader, in fact, he was a better one than Dad ever could've been. When he killed Dad and took over I thought we'd be moving into a new era. But he let power get into his head, and he stopped thinking. He listens to recruits and people lower down than him, instead of me, his adviser. He leaves little bits and clues of our whereabouts everywhere that we go. He forces us to rob and steal from other gangs, it's despicable. If we get caught, then there will be a war. And if there's a war, soon enough people who don't need to die will die. Gang wars happen, true. But we shouldn't be starting rivalries right now. If I wasn't his adviser then we already would've been caught. You're his daughter, if you want him out of this business, help me. I don't want to kill him, he's my brother. And if we just get him arrested, then he'd still be the boss, people in the gang would protect him in jail. He would eventually find out that we were scheming. People outside of the jail would come after us. You know him, you can do something."

He looks at me and sighs, stopping at a red light, he unties the rope binding my hands. When the light turns green again, he rushes through the empty street. I have an overwhelming urge to scratch my head, wondering why he bothered to stop at the red light when he was just going to speed through the street after it turned green.

We're both silent for a while, I'm staring out the window at the dark sky. The moon is glimmering with the stolen light from the sun, and it's beautiful. He clears his throat and drives towards the back of some grungy and old looking stores.

"I can keep him safe, your boyfriend, I mean."

What does he mean? He wouldn't be able to do anything to protect him. How would he even convince my dad not to hurt him?

He makes a sharp right turn into an alley, and I gasp when he stops the car.

"Dad promised not to hurt him as long as I didn't turn the files into the police." I say, my voice shaking with uncertainty. Uncle Xavier raises his eyebrows at me, he even smirks.

"I thought you were smart, Seline." He says, and I lower my head to look at the floor. "Even if you don't turn it in, he'll be watching you and your boyfriend for a long time. One day he'll decide it's better to just kill you both and get rid of the evidence than leave a liability alone. You think he really cares about you so much that he'd ignore you threatening him? That's not how the world works, darling."

I sigh and nod my head, I should've known that already. He knows where Austen lives. He could kill him as a way to punish me for not listening to him. I just thought that he would want me to be happy. I thought he'd want to leave me alone. I guess I was wrong to think something like that.

"I'm sorry, I'm not naive, I promise. It's just hard, I thought I was doing what was right, but I was careless."

His eyes soften and he smiles. I've never seen Uncle Xavier smile: he smirks, glares, and scowls, but he hasn't smiled in front of me, till now. His smile makes me relax into the uncomfortable leather seat.

"You're a teenager, your father didn't bring you up in the Mists. It's normal to believe that the world can give you a break. But don't make that mistake again, the world isn't easy. It doesn't give free handouts. Not all human beings care about other people besides themselves. People like me, we kill for sport; we don't feel remorse and we get what we want. Even now, I kidnapped a teenage girl, punched her, and I did it to force her to help me. And I would do it again. I'm not a knight in shining armor, but I swore to Sean that I'd protect you no matter what. I'm thinking that means I can protect you from him too."

Taking his keys out of the ignition, he walks out of the car, he opens my car door and unties my legs. He grabs my arm and drags me towards a black door in the alley. I don't say a word as he sticks his keys into the locked door.

The door opens and my jaw drops in astonishment as I admire the interior of the building. The walls are a beautiful and elegant teal. The floor is shiny and spotless, and there is a golden, shimmering chandelier hanging from the ceiling. A large stage is positioned near the back of the room, next to the stairs. Fancy circular tables are set up, surrounding the stage. He drags me up the stairs, and we walk up at least two flights.

When we reach a wooden door, he slides another pair of keys into the door handle and we walk into the small room. I walk ahead and sit in a comfortable looking chair, when I hear the lock click behind me.

He sits in a chair in front of mine, and he sighs.

"This place is beautiful. How did you come across it?" I ask, my curiosity in the place grows as I look around the small room. It isn't as lavish as the room downstairs, but it's still gorgeous. There are black bookshelves covering the whole right side of the walls. A wooden desk with a black laptop sitting in between them. A gorgeous crystal lantern hangs in the middle of the room, and I'm breathless.

"It's one of the Mists old clubs; when the prohibition act was signed, our gang was one of the many gangs that made illegal clubs so that we could sell our alcohol. It's a small and ugly apartment, police would never have been able to guess that people were partying in here."

I smile as I imagine the people who came to this place. I can imagine them whispering the secret password, coming into the room, and dancing the night away to soulful music. I can imagine how alive it must've felt dancing here. I can imagine how freeing women must've felt, wearing short dresses without being judged and drinking the night away.

"Now, Seline, we need to come up with a plan." He says, shattering my illusion.

Chapter 24

"I KNOW YOU DON'T LIKE TO BEAT AROUND THE BUSH AND everything, but, can't we just take a quick breather?"

Uncle Xavier glares at me, nostrils flaring, and he rubs the top of his shaved head.

"You're kidding right?" He asks. "We don't have time to sit, relax, and sip some tea, kid. Your dad could call me in to help him any minute now." I sigh and nod my head. Rubbing my sore back, I wince.

"We could let Austen and his family stay here. It's big enough right?"

"Well, I guess. There are two bedrooms up here and I could try and sneak two beds downstairs."

I smile and run my hands through my messy hair.

"Now getting my dad out of the equation is the hard part."

Just the thought of hurting my dad makes me cringe. I bite my lip and pull at my hair in frustration as I try to figure out how to do this without hurting my dad.

"How hard would it be to return all of the money back to the gangs without Dad noticing?" I ask, small ideas beginning to bubble up in the back of my mind. If Dad doesn't notice the money is missing then we can set up a trap. We could tell the gangs that Dad was the one who stole from him. As soon as the thought runs through my head, shut it down. It isn't an option. Although, the plan might work. The gang would kill him for it.

"Impossible, he'll know that the money is gone the moment he tries to spend it." He scoffs. "And even if he doesn't figure it out, it wouldn't matter, he would just steal the money back again."

"If we set up a trap for him then he wouldn't be able to." I bite my nails. "But they would kill him, wouldn't they?"

"Yes." He says without even blinking and I groan in desperation. "But then what exactly could we do?" I'm starting to worry, what will happen when he realizes that I can't help him? Will he refuse to help protect Austen?

"Have you seen a ring with the initials CS, engraved onto it?" I ask, remembering the ring that Austen told me about in his story. I still don't understand why exactly someone would rob a place like that but only want to take a ring. Apparently, they still have the ring too so I'm worried it could have something to do with the Mists. My intuition could be wrong and all but if it does then that means that someone in my family could be responsible for all of Austen's trauma.

Uncle Xavier scowls at me and leans forward on his seat. His harsh glare reminds me that I shouldn't be sitting so comfortably in this room. He punched me in my back and forced me into his car a couple of minutes ago.

"Yes, I have. It has nothing to do with our situation right now but why do you know about that? We lost it to some rich family ages ago. One of our lackeys got caught looking for him and is still in jail right now."

"Someone tried to rob Austen's house when they were younger and apparently all they were after was a ring. But if it's really important to my dad then maybe we can use it to bribe him. We could take it and-"

"We're not touching that damned ring!" He shouts, his fists balling up at his sides and his jaw clenching up. "That ring isn't going anywhere. Leave it with your boyfriend's family. It has no meaning for the gang."

"Oh." I whisper. "Can I ask you why you're so angry about it then? I just don't understand what's so special about that ring." I say quietly.

His face softens a little bit and he takes a long deep breath.

"Fine," he says. "It belonged to my dad's best friend, Chad Stanfield, who got the ring on his wedding day. The ring was stolen by a man named Max Jacobs. My dad trusted Max, he saw a lot of himself in him, but Uncle Chad hated Max. Chad thought he was unreliable, stupid, arrogant, and dishonest. But since Dad trusted Max, Chad had to deal with it. No one, except Dad, was surprised when Max was arrested for working with an opposing gang, apparently, he went down for attempted murder on some woman named Lia Hamilton. Chad didn't tell anyone that Max stole his ring. But a couple of people in the gang started getting suspicious because he kept going to the prison to visit Max, and because he kept going back to the place where Max was arrested. Chad's wife died of cancer that year and Chad broke down. He didn't talk to anyone and he was always out looking for his ring. Whenever he was with the gang in the mansion, he locked himself in his room and sobbed. He killed himself a year later. My dad took me to come and get him, but instead of finding him passed out on the bed like we usually did, we found Chad's suicide note and his dead body lie on his bed next to an empty pill bottle. That was the first time I ever saw my dad cry. My dad spent his entire life looking for that ring. He swore up and down that he would avenge his best friend, my uncle. My dad even died before he could fulfill that promise. It was around the time that he sent someone to try and rob Aiden and Lia Hendrikson's house Sean put a bullet in Dad's head. Dad had been too preoccupied with that stupid ring that people began questioning whether or not he could be a good leader. He had to go."

He clears his throat and looks me dead in the eyes. I feel sympathy for grandpa but at the same time I feel guilty for feeling like that. Grandpa wasn't exactly a good person either… I sigh, picking at my nails as I try to figure out what exactly I'm supposed to be feeling.

"Don't ask your boyfriend for that stupid ring, okay?" I raise an eyebrow at him. Really?

"It has no use, your dad won't give a shit about it and the people who were related to it are either dead or gone or in prison."

"He isn't my boyfriend. I just thought that you should know that." I say with a laugh. "Seriously, don't call him that."

Uncle Xavier smirks at me, leaning back into his chair.

"But you knew who I was talking about, right? If he isn't your boyfriend then you want him to be."

I blush in embarrassment. Even my uncle can tell how much I like Austen. Why do I have to be so transparent? I cough and try to change the conversation.

"So, if we can't use the ring, what can we do? How do we get Dad to step away from his position?" I groan and try to think of what my dad loves more than power. At first I thought it was his family. But that isn't true at all; he ditched his family to become the boss of the Mists and he's enjoying himself in that position. He said he couldn't have given that title to Uncle Xavier, but he seems more qualified for the job than my dad.

"I have an idea." He says. His frustrating smirk grew wider on his face. "Listen up, because this is going to get complicated."

Chapter 25

IT'S BEEN A WEEK SINCE UNCLE XAVIER AND I CAME UP WITH A PLAN. Austen and I are closer now, we're more friendly than flirty, and I have no idea why.

I miss his gaze and his touch. I miss him. He's sitting on his bed with my laptop, and even though he's here with me, I want more of him. My heart clenches inside my chest whenever I think about him. I know that I shouldn't really be worrying about being in a relationship right now, but I can't help it.

When I look into his eyes, my heart drops into my stomach. When he speaks to me, his voice low and seductive, my body calls for him. When I'm scared, I want to stop wasting time and jump into his arms.

"Aus, I'm going to leave if you don't give me back my laptop."

Even right now, while we're just sitting and joking around together, I want him to hold me and kiss me. He pouts and looks at me with adorable puppy dog eyes.

"I just wanted to help my girl get the pathetic teenage girls off of her back. What do you find fun about answering these questions anyway?" He raises his hands in defeat.

I smile and my heartbeat quickens. He just called me his girl. I'm his girl. Giggling, I watch him as he gets off his bed and smirks. He stalks towards me, his feet hitting the wooden floor as he makes his way to the desk chair I'm sitting on.

"I'm your girl now?" I ask, crossing my arms against my chest. I try to make my voice sound incredulous and bored, but you can hear the pathetic hope in it.

He glares at me. A passionate and alluring fire burning beneath the depths of his gorgeous brown eyes. He bends down to meet my eyes.

"You have been mine since the very first day I met you, little Sel." He hisses. "The first day that I laid my eyes on you; the first moment you spoke to me, you've been mine. You have always been on my mind and I know I've been on yours. You. Are. My. Girl. You always have been. Don't fool yourself into thinking otherwise."

"Don't be all condescending, Aus. I haven't always been your girl. You got around while I was free and single. You didn't even notice me until you wanted your sister to be with your best friend. You only seemed interested when you needed me."

He holds my face in his hands and looks at me, eyes wide, looking like he wants to shake me.

"Says who?! Sure, I've been with other girls. You're right about that, but I haven't been with a lot of them. Don't tell me I haven't noticed you before I talked to you either because it's just not true. Think about it, little Sel. How the hell did I even know who to go to to help me with my sister? I don't have people that I talk to in school, most people are afraid of me. I don't listen to gossip or rumors, and I have no idea who anyone is at that school besides Corbin and Lissa anyway. But I knew your name, and I knew where your locker was. The Christian girl in the classroom who only talks to people when they want advice. The girl with such a big heart and no one to share it with. I noticed you Ms. Perfect, I did. I just stayed away."

"I don't believe you," I whisper, leaning into his palm. "Even if what you're saying is true that doesn't change the fact that even though you say, 'I'm your girl'-" I use my fingers to make air quotes. "You haven't done a single thing about it. You haven't asked me out. You haven't kissed me since last week. You said you love me, and then acted like we were just friends a week later."

"Because you're putting your life in danger and I'm scared! Until I know that all of this bullshit is over, I'm not doing anything. Your going to go through this stupid plan no matter what I say, and I don't want to get everything that I want and lose it in a matter of minutes."

"Aus, the plan is safe, it's foolproof. Don't do anything stupid, please," he scowls at me.

"You're going to bring your lunatic dad inside my house and turn his whole gang against him. Excuse me for caring about your safety enough to realize how foolish that is. What if he decides to go in, guns blazing? Huh? How are you going to protect yourself?"

What he doesn't understand is that if I can get my dad to confess that he lost his touch as the leader. If I can get him to explain that all of the time away from the gang made him forget how to run one without causing unnecessary wars, then I can record it and send it to my Uncle Xavier. He'll be in the middle of a meeting with his gang about my dad and how he needs to be stopped. He'll have evidence that even my dad agrees that he shouldn't be in charge. The plan is genius. We can get my dad safe and tucked away in jail, without any influence from the gang, and with my uncle in charge of the new gang he can get people to back off of my dad. Once he's separated from the gang we can send him to prison and he won't be able to get out or be protected by people inside the system. We need to do this, it's important.

"He's my dad. He isn't going to hurt me. I'll be safe, I promise. This is the only way to do this without anyone dying."

"He's your dad, you're right, but he abandoned you. He hurt your mom. He kidnapped you, and he threatened you. I don't doubt that he would try to do it again." He strokes my cheeks and kisses me. His soft lips caressing mine for a quick moment before he pulls back to look at me.

"Let me ask my mom for help. She has connections with people who probably know how to deal with this better."

"My dad will put a target on her back for it. I'm not letting your mom risk her life for me."

"He has connections that won't just disappear in jail, little Sel. He could hire people to hurt you."

"He wouldn't be able to do that if he's removed from his position though. Uncle Xavier will take over seamlessly and then we can get him in prison without any trouble." I sigh and press our lips together. "You have to let me do this."

"I'm pretty sure I love you, Aus," I whisper, standing up and heading towards his temporary bedroom door.

"That's how me and you are different, I know I love you." I freeze, trying not to turn around and look back at him and then I quietly walk out of the room and head down the stairs. I take my phone out of my pocket and send a text to my dad.

'Meet me at Austen's house. Be there by 8.' Then without looking back, I walk out the door.

I decide to take extra precautions when I get to Austen's house. Taking Austen's words to heart, I lock every single door, besides the front door, and all the windows inside the house. I hide every single weapon that my dad could use on me if he gets his hands on it. I find myself staring at a pocket knife, I have a feeling that he's going to do something. This gut feeling that something is about to go wrong. So I grab the pocket knife, hiding in my back jeans pocket.

It's about seven forty five, and I text my uncle and tell him to start the meeting soon. I spin the phone around my fingers and wait. Till finally, I hear a knock on the door. It's showtime. I turn the recorder on my phone on, put the phone in my back pocket, and open the door for my dad.

"Why did you call me out here Seline?" Dad asks me and the cold look in his eyes makes me flinch.

"Let's talk upstairs. Come with me." I gesture for him to follow me with my hands and head to Mrs. Hendrickson's room.

When he walks into the room he starts to look around. He seems a bit suspicious of me and he should be.

"Come home," I say and my voice sounds sad and quiet. "You don't even like the gang and you don't have to be in it."

"Seline, we've talked about this already," he sighs. "I'm doing this for my dad."

"Uncle Xavier can do it, Dad. He's grandpa's kid too. Plus, he's been with the gang for years so he knows what he's doing."

"It's my responsibility, Kiddo." He says with a smile, ruffling up my hair. I try not to remember how he used to do that when I was little. I try not to remember the nickname he used to call me.

"But you aren't even doing well! It must be so tiring, and I don't think that it's worth it. You've stooped so low Dad; you even steal from other gangs now. Wouldn't that start a war?"

"You don't think I know that," he shouts. "Sorry, I didn't mean to shout at you. The job is exhausting. And you're right, I'm doing a terrible job. Because of me, there'll probably be a war by next year, and I don't know what the hell I'm doing. But I can't just give up. My dad died for this, and if I have to, I'll die too. Proudly." I flinch, he'd die for the gang. Of course he would, he'd protect the gang before his family any day.

"I'm sorry Dad, I didn't mean to upset you."

"It's okay, but I have to leave now. I have something that I need to do. I'm glad that we could meet out here, but I'm not stupid. I know nothing's changed between us." When he leaves the room, I stop the recording and text it to Uncle Xavier.

He freezes and looks at me suspiciously.

"Who the fuck did you just text?!"

He tries to grab me and I try to break it to the door. He grabs me and I scream.

"Let me go!"

"Do you think I'm dumb? I was suspicious of you from the start. Answer my fucking question Seline!"

I scream for help but there's no one inside this house that can help me. Austen and his family are all in the empty club that Uncle Xavier showed me. I wince as I try to reach for the pocket knife and I slash at his arms with it. He lets me go, grabbing onto his bleeding arm and I run out of the room. I head all the way downstairs as fast as I can and I run out of the front door. I'm surprised to see Mr. Hendrikson in a fancy car just sitting there. I knock on the passenger door only to see my dad rushing out behind me with his bleeding arm.

Mr. Hendrikson gestures for me to hurry inside and when I do I sigh in relief. Thank God that he was here to get me out of this place.

"Austen told me it could get dangerous, I'm glad he did too. We were all worried about you."

"Thanks for saving me, Mr Hendrikson."

"Well, we weren't gonna' make a little girl make such dangerous moves on her own. If I knew you were going to confront your dad by yourself beforehand we wouldn't have just stayed in a temporary place like that. We would've confronted him on our own. We're a pretty powerful family Seline, we didn't need you to do this."

"Maybe so, but he's still my dad… I needed to do this on my own."

The ride back to the empty club was silent. It was a comfortable silence that made me feel like everything was finally over for good. While I was in the care I called the police and sent over the files that incriminated my father and I prayed that they'd find him soon. When we finally get to the empty club, I rush out the car.

I run as fast as I can to Austen, and when I get there I'm breathing heavily. I'm finally free to be whoever I want. I'm free. My heart beats inside my chest, as my feet carry me into his room and I swing his door open. He's standing up next to the bed and I lunge at him. Both our bodies collapse onto the soft mattress, and I fist the hair on the back of his neck.

"My part in the plan is over. We don't have to wait for anything anymore. Uncle Xavier will pull through with the rest."

"Be my girlfriend, little Sel," he whispers against my lips and I shiver. "Be mine."

"It took you long enough," I chuckle. "But, yeah, I think I'd be okay with that."

<h1 style="text-align:center">Epilogue</h1>

AUSTEN'S POV

I'M HAPPY. I'VE BEEN SO FUCKING HAPPY THESE PAST FEW YEARS, so disgustingly happy, and, still, I'm not used to it. I'm not used to smiling every day. I'm not used to feeling like I could touch the stars. I'm not used to having hope. I'm not used to someone making me feel like I can be a good person.

Today's the day that I look at the woman of my dreams and drop down on one knee I've never been so scared in my damn life.

"Kaden, come on man..." I mutter to myself. He promised that he would be here to give me the finishing touches I need to actually get her to say yes.

"I'm right here idiot," he says, smacking me over my head. "Dude, why are you sweating so hard? I know you're nervous, but this is kind of extreme. Calm down, I doubt you want to smell like B.O when you propose to her. This is why I'm not about to propose to Zoey anytime soon, Austen. I already act like an idiot around her, I don't need to make myself look like I'm more of a jackass than usual."

I tug at my tie, sweat drips down my forehead, and I wipe it away. My hair must look ridiculous right now. I groan, she's definitely going to say no to me.

"Is it getting hot in here, or is it just me?"

"Dude, like I said, it's just your nerves. Calm down."

Normally, I'd punch him in the throat for trying to tell me what to do, but lately we've been getting along. I remember the day he came knocking on my apartment door trying to apologize to me. His girlfriend, Zoey, was the one who brought him down here. Opening the car door, I take deep breaths to try and relax. I need to calm down. She isn't going to say yes to me if I look like a scared, sweaty puppy.

I sit down inside the comfy, tan car and smile. I'm at her favorite place, the lake beside her church, sitting in a rented, black, 1967 Chevy Impala, her favorite car.

The car is a piece of crap but she likes it because of some stupid show that she's hooked on. I think it's called Supernatural?

Whatever, I sit inside the car with my asshole brother, who keeps talking.

"And, come on, why settle on this chick, Austen? She's kind of cute and all, but she's got a lot of emotional baggage."

I turn around and glare at him.

"Who the fuck do you think you are? I asked for your help because you're my brother. All I wanted you to get was the damn Impala and then leave. If you're going to stay, then don't you ever say a word about Sel. She's everything to me and I won't toler-" before I can finish speaking I see Sel walking out of the church with her mom. She looks gorgeous. She's wearing a pale pink dress that flows to her knees. It accentuates all of her curves. Her hair is down and waving down her back like water.

"Wow," I whisper. My eyes are drinking her in. She walks seductively towards the lake. Her legs are long and tan. Gosh, she's perfect.

She lays down in the grass and stares up into the sky. Her skin glows as the sun hits her, I gulp. How the hell am I supposed to propose to her when she always looks like a damn goddess!?

I glare at her and stomp out of the door, slamming it shut. She jumps, looking up into my direction. She smiles at me, and I glare at her.

"Is that what I think it is!?" She squeals, and I sigh. "Is that a 1967 Chevy Impala?!" She questions, and I ignore her.

"What are you wearing?" I ask, her smile fades. She glares right back at me.

"Excuse me?" She asks, one eyebrow raised. I try not to look intimidated, but she's probably the only person in the universe I've ever been intimidated by.

"I'm sorry, I'm just nervous. I have something I want to ask you and it's hard to keep focus when you look so gorgeous."

She smiles, and I grab her hand. "Yes that is what you think it is," I say. "It's a 1967 Chevy Impala, and I'll buy it for you if you marry me."

At first, I wasn't planning on bribing her, but I'm not very romantic, and I don't want her to say no.

"You wanna repeat that?" She asks, but when she turns around, I'm already kneeling on the ground.

"I love you so much, Sel, and I want to spend the rest of my life with you. Please, baby girl, marry me and make me the happiest man in the world." I heard that "make me the happiest guy in the world" crap from a movie and it rang true to me. I would be as happy as I could get if she agreed to marry me.

I fish out the diamond ring that I bought for her, a couple of days ago, out of my pocket and open the little black box.

She smiles, her eyes filled with unshed tears, and I close the box.

"It's okay, don't cry. I'm sorry. I didn't mean to pressure you or anything. You can say no, I'll wait till you're ready." I stand up and try to put my arms around her, but she slaps me. I press my hand to my stinging cheek and raise my eyebrows in shock.

"Of course I'll marry you, you idiot!" She shouts. "You didn't need to try and bribe me," she rolls her eyes. "I would've still said yes."

I wrap my arms around her and hug her, lifting her up off the ground and spinning her around. Her beautiful little giggles ring in my ears, I never want to put her down. She's breathless and panting when I finally put her on the ground.

We smile at each other, our eyes locked onto one another's. I pull the white box out of my pocket again, and open it. I slide the small ring on her finger, knowing that we're going to be spending the rest of our lives together, helps me breathe. I feel alive.

"I love you," I whisper to her, and she smiles at me. Her whole face brightening up, her bright eyes hypnotizing me.

"I love you too." My heart pounds and shakes inside of my chest. Kaden's standing off to the side, staring at us with a smile. Mrs. Winters is standing by her car, watching us too. Normally when people stare at me, I get furious. But with my fiancé in my arms, the world just stops. And, suddenly, I'm free.

~END~

Bonus Chapter

After living together with Austen for some time and now being married to him I've come to the realization that he might be more insecure than I am. He's one of the sweetest people I've ever met in my entire life, and he just doesn't see it. He's smarter than he thinks he is too. When we were in college together, he got better grades in school than me. He's neat, he doesn't leave messes all over the place. He's a lot like his mom.

We go to family celebrations together and we just hang out with his entire family and me and my mom. I've never felt so loved in my entire life than when I'm around his family. Especially while being around so many lovely couples who you can look at and just tell how in love they are. Kaden is as sweet around his girlfriend Zoey as usual. Allisa and Corbin are finally together and they're sickeningly adorable. He's always holding her and trying to hug her from behind. It's cute. Kale and Jensen are as lovey-dovey as ever, and even Mr. Hendrikson and Ms. Lia are always together and flirting.

Austen's been in therapy for years now and he's learned how to be calm around his family members now. He's never been aggressive with me but when he was around his family… I can't say that he was always on his best behavior.

I've seen a lot of fights with him and his brothers when we were just dating and they weren't pretty. I saw him punch Kaden at one point, his brother kind of deserved it but again, it wasn't a good look. I'm glad that we've moved past that though. Now they get into arguments occasionally but it's never too serious.

He showers me with so much love that I feel like I'm dreaming most days. When we fight it's usually over stupid stuff like not being able to go on dates or what we'll name our first child. Life is amazing for us.

"Austen, are you working tomorrow night?!" I yell from the living room sofa. He decided that he would cook for me tonight and I'm very excited. He makes an amazing alfredo and I'm always so in love with his food.

"I already told you I'm not," he yells back and I smile.

"Then let's go have a picnic! It's gonna' be really warm tomorrow."

"Hmmm, that sounds fun. If we have any leftovers tonight we could take some Alfredo tomorrow too."

I head to the kitchen when the delicious smell of food starts to become unbearable for me.

"I'm so hungry," I groan. "I want that food in my belly right now!"

"Fine, here you go you little brat!" We both laugh as he puts two plates of food on our kitchen table.

I twirl the pasta around my fork and moan at the delicious taste of his food entering my mouth. He always keeps me so satisfied and happy. I can't help but smile.

"It tastes delicious as always, Aus."

"You only call me that when I feed you," he rolls his eyes with a little smile on his face.

"You know I kinda miss when you called me, little Sel. It's always Seline or Sel now. What happened to the little part?"

"Hmmm, really I thought you hated all that."

"I didn't like it when you called me Ms. Perfect. I had no problems with little Sel."

He laughs, the sound echoing in the room and I can't help but smile at the sound.

"I guess I wasn't as bad at nicknames as I thought."

"Guess not."

We crack a few more jokes together as we eat and we have so much fun that we're sitting there for a while even after we ate all of our food. We decide that I'll wash the dishes since he made the food and then when we're all done, I head to the shower to get ready for bed.

"Do you mind if I join you?"

"The doctor said that it isn't good for my body to have sex while pregnant for the first three months. We're in month two, don't push your luck."

"We don't have to have sex, I could just help you clean up…"

"Nope, you'll shower after me."

"Alright, fine."

We both laugh and I feel so happy and content. One day I'll meet my baby and we'll be onto the newest chapter of our lives together. I honestly couldn't be more excited.

"I love you, Aus."

"Love you too, little Sel."